OPHELIA'S WAR: DANGEROUS MERCY

RUBIES OF RUIN, BOOK TWO

Ophelia's War: Dangerous Mercy

Alison L. McLennan

FIVE STAR
A part of Gale, a Cengage Company

Farmington Hills, Mich • San Francisco • New York • Waterville, Maine
Meriden, Conn • Mason, Ohio • Chicago

Five Star Publishing, a part of Gale, a Cengage Company

LIBRARY OF CONGRESS CATALOGING-IN-PUBLICATION DATA

Names: McLennan, Alison L., author.
Title: Ophelia's war : dangerous mercy / Alison L. McLennan.
Other titles: Dangerous mercy
Description: First Edition. | Farmington Hills, Mich. : Five Star, a part of Gale, a Cengage Company, 2019. | Series: Rubies of Ruin ; book 2 | Identifiers: LCCN 2019002966 (print) | ISBN 9781432858148 (hardcover : alk. paper)
Subjects: | GSAFD: Love stories.
Classification: LCC PS3613.C57855 O62 2019 (print) | DDC 813/.6—dc23
LC record available at https://lccn.loc.gov/2019002966

First Edition. First Printing: October 2019
Find us on Facebook—https://www.facebook.com/FiveStarCengage
Visit our website—http://www.gale.cengage.com/fivestar
Contact Five Star Publishing at FiveStar@cengage.com

Printed in Mexico
1 2 3 4 5 6 7 23 22 21 20 19

To my mother for her unbridled encouragement
and persistent promotion of my work.
And to Mick, I hope this story captures your attention
and imagination as much as Poldark.

ACKNOWLEDGMENTS

Many thanks to Tiffany Schofield, Alice Duncan, Erin Bealmear, and the team at Five Star for publication and editorial support. My most humble gratitude goes to the cosmic forces, which in the midst of this project allowed me a brief glimpse into the beyond and forever transformed me. And to my readers, without you there'd be nothing.

One

Grafton, Utah, 1884

The graveyard was the only part of Grafton that had grown. Etched into stone were the names of Mary York, the Berry brothers, and Ophelia's friends: Letty and Lizzy Russell. Ophelia placed her hand on the sisters' headstone and was surprised by its warmth. The girls had been flying through the air on the swing down by the cotton gin and singing silly variations of church hymns in loud giggly voices. They didn't hear the tree branch creak and groan before it snapped. Their skinny entwined bodies crashed upon the earth and, just like that, they were gone.

Was it bad luck? Or was Grafton cursed? Many settlers had died in peculiar circumstances over a short time span. Ophelia's parents had succumbed to a fever. There'd been no doctor, so she didn't know if the fever was scarlet, or yellow, or some other sort. The settlers had all proclaimed it was a miracle that she and her brother, Ezekiel, hadn't been infected.

There'd been people even unluckier than her parents and the Russell girls; people who couldn't be properly buried. In the spring of sixty-two, when the first settlers arrived, it rained nonstop for forty days. Ellen Tenny was giving birth in the family wagon-box when a flash flood swept the wagon away. Mr. Tenny had run for help and returned to find the Virgin River had taken his makeshift home, his wife, and his half-born child.

After tending her garden, Ophelia would often watch the

evening sun dance on the water and think about Mrs. Tenny and her baby, amazed at how the river could both give and take away life.

She made her way toward her parents' graves and glanced around for her uncle's, hoping he wasn't buried too close to them. Shooting him hadn't been easy for her to live with. She often woke from a recurring nightmare featuring blood dripping from the ceiling and seeping through the floor of their old cabin. If there was a hell, it might be where she would go upon her own death. Sometimes it felt as though she was there already. A large coiled rattlesnake slept in the sand in front of William Hastings's headstone. Charlie saw it and reached for his knife. Ophelia squeezed his arm and gave him a disapproving look.

She whispered, "It's bad luck to kill anything in a graveyard. Besides, he's just sleeping."

In the distance, a flustered Mrs. Thompson hurried up the dirt road toward them. She stopped for a minute, put her hands on her knees, caught her breath, and continued her march. Ophelia, Ezekiel, and Charlie had made the mistake of riding in plain sight right past Mrs. Thompson's homestead. Ophelia sighed and watched with dread as the woman approached.

Mrs. Thompson pushed open the gate and fumbled to close it behind her. Filled with what seemed unfitting jubilance, considering the setting, she spoke to Ophelia as if she were bearing wonderful news. "Ophelia Oatman! It *is* you. Why, I'd recognize that bright orange hair anywhere. How on earth did you survive your kidnapping? Does your uncle know you're alive? I want to hear the whole story."

Mrs. Thompson's words stunned Ophelia. Everything around her intensified: the sun bore down hotter; insects buzzed louder; a faint but persistent drumming pounded in her head. In order to stand straight, Ophelia anchored her gaze on Mrs. Thompson. But the vertical grooves around Mrs. Thompson's lips and the layer of white gathered in the corners of her mouth only made Ophelia more unsteady. She attempted to ignore the chaos of sensations, the heaviness of her head, and the pull of the earth beckoning her body. She transferred her gaze from Mrs. Thompson's mouth straight into her eyes. "My uncle?" asked Ophelia. "Why, he's dead."

Mrs. Thompson blinked, paused, and seemed to be searching her memory for missed gossip. She addressed Ophelia in the sweet yet patronizing tone of an elder sister. That tone reminded Ophelia of all those claustrophobic winter quilting bees when the elder sisters had to constantly correct her clumsy hands. She felt a strange mix of nostalgia and nausea.

"Your uncle is alive and well. Oh, my, you poor creature, did you think he'd been killed during the robbery? He was shot in the arm, and he would have bled to death if the blessed Widow Hopkins hadn't found him and nursed him back to health." Mrs. Thompson smiled and lowered her voice. "They fell in love and got married. Why, he's one of us now. He's a Saint! And for nearly a decade, he's been searching the territory for you. Everyone in Grafton assumed you were the dead one. We all thought he was foolish to keep looking. But we admired his devotion and duty."

Stunned into silence, Ophelia felt her body waver. Her head felt like a lead ball, and she could hardly bear the weight of it. She held onto Charlie's arm to help her remain upright. How could her uncle be alive? She'd shot him herself, and then seen him lying still as a stone in a puddle of blood. Clutching Charlie, she steadied herself and digested the news.

For over a decade, she'd been plagued with guilt and nightmares. But she hadn't killed her Uncle Luther after all. Relief swept over her, and then her throat felt tight, as if his hands were around her neck, trying to choke her and steal the ruby necklace. If he was alive, he could find her and hurt her again. She removed her hand from Charlie's arm and quickly tucked the ruby necklace under her dress collar out of *Sister* Thompson's prying gaze.

Even though Ophelia couldn't recall her exact state of mind when she'd shot her uncle, she knew she had meant to kill him. Violated and scared, she'd had no more sense than a trapped animal. He had stolen the jewel of her virginity and ruined her for a decent life. Certainly, shooting him had to be an excusable sin, considering the rape. In terms of sin, her lust and years of whoring had never concerned her as much as had her uncle's killing.

She'd fare much better on judgment day now that she knew she hadn't killed her kin. It would be easier if there was no judgment, and, as Charlie believed, we turned to dirt. Or maybe—and the thought often caused her to smile—God would turn out to be a woman. There'd be a lot of men in a heap of trouble if God turned out to be a woman. But man had created God in his image, and therefore God could not possibly be a woman. Anyone suggesting so would be branded a heretic and ostracized. She'd already been labeled a morally bankrupt harlot and didn't want to be further scorned for blasphemy, so she gave her thoughts no tongue and put them from her mind.

Of course, there was still the problem of Red Farrell, the other man she'd killed. She'd given him fair warning, but he'd lunged at her anyway, despite the gun pointed at his face. His unexpected laughter echoed in her memory. He'd laughed so hard, tears had rolled down his mangled face. She had watched him dying, emitting hoots and howls, quaking with both hilarity and pain. When he finally expired, she'd removed his boots and valuables and dragged his body into the river, trying to convince herself it was his hysteria that had killed him and not the bullet she'd fired into his face.

A hot wind kicked up dirt devils and swirled sand into her

eyes. She squeezed them shut to stop the grit from scratching her eyeballs, then opened them slowly and stared down at his boots. After all those years, they still graced her feet. Soft and worn, they fit like a second skin. He'd had small feet, and his boots had fit her better than the worn-out shoes she'd been wearing that day. But there was no need to keep wearing them. She had plenty of others. If she could stop wearing his boots, maybe his ghost would finally disappear. But she couldn't. And sometimes Red Farrell's presence would hover around her thoughts, like an uninvited party guest milling around a banquet table.

Another wave of unsteadiness hit, and she squeezed Charlie's arm so hard, he actually yelped. Even with him at her side, terror filled her. She wasn't the fainting type, but it came as a shock to find out her uncle was alive after she'd believed him dead for so long.

The sun burned her skin straight through her bonnet and dress. She tried to take a deep breath but mostly inhaled dust. She wanted to mount her spotted pony and ride away as fast and far as she could. Mrs. Thompson finished telling them about Luther's conversion to Mormonism and his marriage to the Widow Hopkins.

As soon as Mrs. Thompson arrived, Ophelia's brother, Ezekiel, had retreated to the corner of the graveyard. If Mrs. Thompson recognized him there could be trouble. It'd been nearly ten years since the settlers had run Ezekiel out of town for supposedly colluding with Chief Black Hawk. Ophelia knew the townspeople well enough to know the incident had not been forgotten. The busybody, Mrs. Thompson, craned her neck and turned her meddlesome gaze over toward Ezekiel, who skulked at the edge of the graveyard with his back to them. In trying so hard not to be seen, he appeared a little suspicious. Ophelia fought a mother-bear instinct to pick up a handful of sand and toss it into Mrs. Thompson's eyes. Poor Ezekiel had already suffered too much at the hands of the Mormons.

Charlie was quick to intervene before Ophelia said or did anything stupid. As he addressed Mrs. Thompson, his voice was filled with conspiratorial authority. Even though the graveyard was deserted, he spoke softly, as if someone might overhear them. From his tongue sprang a pack of lies, told with such confidence, Ophelia almost believed them herself.

"Ma'am, I'm a detective. The name's Thomas Green. For a long time, my wife has wanted to pay her respects here at this remote desert graveyard where her parents have been laid to rest. I decided I'd kill two birds while we were out this way and see if I could catch wind of these fellows here—" Charlie reached inside his pocket and produced a handbill. "That Indian"—he motioned to Zeke with a nod of his head—"is my tracker, Dull Knife. He's a good scout, but he's not too fond of palefaces he's not acquainted with, so just keep your distance from him if you don't mind."

Sister Thompson's eyes went wide, and she clutched her throat. "Oh, my laws!" She cast one last curious glance in Zeke's direction before squinting down at the handbill. Because of her constant squinting, Ophelia's concern that she would recognize Zeke diminished some.

"Look closely," said Charlie. "Have you seen either of these men?"

Mrs. Thompson studied the handbill and pointed to one of the men. "He's a handsome lad. I do believe I'd remember him." She shook her head. "No, sorry. I haven't seen either of them. What should I do if they pay a visit?"

Charlie took off his hat and scratched the back of his head. "You could either bar your door and fetch your gun or play ignorant and just offer them refreshment. I don't reckon they'll harm you. They're professional criminals and mostly hold up trains and banks. There's been no reports of them trying to rob settlers. That's why it's been so hard to catch 'em." Charlie glanced around at the modest settlement. Six teepees stood by the river, and a slow-moving Paiute was making his way up the hill toward one of the established brick houses. "There's a lot of Paiute around here. Do they bother you?"

A resigned smile spread across Sister Thompson's face. She sighed and shook her head. "No, they don't bother us. Unlike the Ute, we've always lived peacefully with the Paiute. Oh, they borrow things without asking, but they make many gifts as well. I'll tell you, when all the white men leave to work on the road to Kolob, I feel much safer with the Paiute around. But just when I start to depend on them, they pack everything up and wander off somewheres else." She threw up her hands in a gesture to show how they vanished.

Charlie nodded his understanding, rolled up the handbill, and replaced it in his pocket. Ophelia wondered why Charlie carried a handbill with pictures of wanted men. Had he lied about terminating his employment with the Pinkerton Agency? She watched the Paiutes and noticed their resemblance to the old Indian woman who had once saved her life.

"Where are my manners?" Mrs. Thompson declared. "Why don't you come to my house for some refreshment?"

Ophelia stepped closer to Mrs. Thompson, held her hands, and continued Charlie's lies. "I do appreciate your offer. But I've come all the way from California to pay respects to my parents. Do you mind?"

Mrs. Thompson clutched at Ophelia's hands and looked hopeful. "I understand, dear. Shall we pray together?"

"I'd really like to be alone with them. It's been a very long time. We'll call in at your place in a little while. I just need some quiet first. Would you mind?"

"Celestial sister, if we pray together, our prayers will be

stronger." She looked at Ophelia and Charlie. "Why, I know you've left Zion, but you're still a Saint, aren't you?"

Ophelia smiled tightly and shook her head.

"You must come back to us. For ten years your uncle has been scouring the territory for you. It's no wonder he didn't find you all the way out there in California. Your Uncle Luther is a Saint now! His conversion and baptism . . . why, it was the most beautiful thing. You must at least tell me how he can get in touch with you. It'll mean so much to him."

"Where does he live now?" asked Charlie.

"He moved to the Great Salt Lake Valley—very close to the Beehive House. Can you imagine?"

"No, I can't imagine," said Charlie. "What is the Beehive House? It sounds unpleasant."

Ophelia shot Charlie a stern look. She didn't want to know where Luther lived. She squeezed Mrs. Thompson's hands until her smile disappeared. "Please, I need a little quiet now and some time alone with my parents. This is difficult for me. I experienced much hardship here at this settlement. It's not easy to return."

"Of course, I understand." Sister Thompson removed her hands from Ophelia's grasp, formed a stiff smile, and rubbed them. "Don't forget to stop by for refreshment."

They finally rid themselves of nosy Mrs. Thompson. Ophelia watched her walk down the sandy road surrounded by a salmon-colored cloud of dust. Once she passed the sorghum mill, Ophelia sighed with relief. She turned to Charlie. "Thank God she's gone. To think I could have ended up her sister-wife makes me shudder."

Ezekiel sauntered over from the corner of the cemetery and stood by them with his arms crossed. "So little O, Luther's still alive. I guess you're not the crack shot you thought you were." A slight smile formed on his lips, and he rocked on his heels.

Despite the animosity between Charlie and Zeke, Charlie burst out laughing at Zeke's remark.

They'd been apart almost ten years, but her brother could still get her goat. "Ezekiel, that's not fair. You can't judge me on that. I had to take aim through a chink in the wall."

Zeke's joking smile disappeared. His eyes hardened and narrowed. "Good thing we know where he lives. I owe him a bullet."

Charlie stopped laughing, adopted a serious tone, and confronted Zeke. "I think I better take care of him."

"I'm blood," Zeke said.

Ophelia glared at them both. Frontier justice allowed for a man to avenge his daughter or wife's rapist. But even though he kept referring to himself as such, Charlie wasn't her husband. When her Uncle Luther violated her, her father was dead and her brother had been run out of Grafton, so she figured it had been within her rights to kill him. Many women in similar circumstances took their own lives out of shame. Ophelia had tried. But Luther found her, pulled her from the river, and carried her back to the cabin. He ruined and saved her on the same night.

Ophelia figured a devil like Luther, who would rape a girl for disobedience, was probably meant to be killed. But ten years had passed, and perhaps with Widow Hopkins's stern guidance and lots of pie to replace the whiskey, he had changed his devilish ways and redeemed himself somehow. Either way, she wanted nothing to do with him. All she wanted was to live in peace without violence, fear, revenge, or the need to sell her favors.

"It's my duty and long overdue," Zeke said. He faced Charlie and stood straight, towering over him. Charlie bristled.

Ophelia interrupted their debate before it turned into a fight. "Charlie, is that why you asked where he lives? So you can kill him? I don't want to know where he lives. I don't want to hear any more about him! Neither of you is going to kill him. This isn't some dime-store novel. Whether Luther deserves to die isn't the question. I don't want to see either of you swing. Didn't you hear Sister Thompson? Luther is part of Mormondom now. It would be almost impossible for either of you to kill him without getting yourselves hanged. Besides, maybe the Widow Hopkins has changed his ways."

Zeke grimaced, shook his head, and shuddered. "Being married to Widow Hopkins is more punishment than I'd wish on my worst enemy." He looked down the road toward Mrs. Thompson's place. "She makes that one look like a catch."

"Oh, Ezekiel, Widow Hopkins wasn't that bad. She was the only person in the whole settlement who helped me after the trouble started."

"What about a duel?" asked Charlie.

"No!" Ophelia stared daggers at Charlie. She poked him in the chest with her index finger. "I don't want to hear any more about it. We're going to bury the hatchet and return to Ogden, where I'd like to live peacefully with my brother." She flattened her hand and patted his chest in a conciliatory gesture. "You're welcome to stay with us, Charlie, if you wish. But before we leave this graveyard, you and Ezekiel must both swear oaths that you will not seek vengeance for my honor."

Charlie and Zeke exchanged glances. Zeke sighed, grimaced, and studied something on the hillside. Charlie chewed his mustache.

"We will stay here all night if that's what it takes." Ophelia crossed her arms and waited. Neither man moved nor spoke. "Ezekiel, swear on our parents' graves." She looked at the sand mounds with the worn wooden crosses over them and back at him.

"Ophelia—I can't."

"You can and you will. There will be no bloodshed for my honor. It's long gone now and not worth defending. Please." She knelt and brushed sand from the old crosses.

Zeke looked down and held up his right hand. "I swear I won't shed any blood in Ophelia's name, Indian's honor."

Ophelia stood and eyed him, wondering if he was being sarcastic. Instead of pursuing her suspicion, she turned her attention toward Charlie. "Chas, it's your turn."

He looked down at the graves. "I wasn't acquainted with your parents. Do you think—"

She threw up her hands. "Then swear on your precious pearl-handled Colt."

He pursed his lips and put his hand on it protectively. "My Colt .45?"

"That's the one."

After some coaxing, Charlie finally swore on his Colt that he wouldn't avenge Luther's crime. Ophelia was tempted to bury the ruby necklace, which had caused so much trouble, in the sand with her parents. But she figured as soon as she left, the constable of ravens that loved shiny objects and kept watch from the height of a nearby cottonwood tree would come and dig it up. She didn't care if a raven flew off with the necklace. But she couldn't bear the thought of a settler from Grafton finding it.

They left the graveyard, mounted their horses, and rode past Sister Thompson's place toward their old homestead. The ravens squawked and cawed. Ophelia turned and saw their dark shapes descending from the cottonwood tree and perching on the tombstones.

Ophelia and Zeke had wanted to replace the flimsy wooden crosses over their parents' graves with a nice engraved stone. But after the encounter with Mrs. Thompson, they thought it best to keep moving. Their old homestead was in a sad, picked-over state. The sight of it brought back too much suffering, so they didn't linger long. Most everything of value had been taken long ago. Ophelia plied a tattered queen of hearts from under a rotten piece of timber. She picked it up, pinched it between her index finger and thumb, held it up to the sun, stared at it for a moment, and then tossed it over her shoulder. It landed in a pile of meaningless debris that was once their youth. Whoever had held the queen of hearts had probably thought he had a lucky hand, before the bullet hit.

Ophelia mounted her horse, took one last look around, and tried to remember the lean but happy times she'd once had with her family prior to her parents' death and her uncle's arrival. She, Charlie, and Zeke rode down to the river and filled their canteens. The horses drank. In an overgrown cottonwood tree, Ophelia's old swing still hung and swayed in the breeze as if a girl was in it. The swing had risen with the growing tree and hung ten feet above the ground.

After Lizzy and Letty had fallen to their deaths from the swing at the cotton gin, Ophelia's father had wanted to cut down her swing. She had begged and pleaded with him to leave it. Finally, he relented. But to ensure her safety, he had climbed the tree and moved the swing to a thicker, more secure branch.

Ophelia figured if a girl could die doing something as innocent as playing on her swing, then nothing in the world could protect her.

Two

They avoided the stage road and traveled a long winding back way to the railroad terminus at Frisco, just in case the posse that had chased them out of Silver Reef was still tracking them. Ophelia didn't say anything, but she had a bad feeling that Ezekiel had started a fire—probably his last job to repay his debt to Mr. Gee. Never mind the property damage. If someone had been killed, there'd be hell to pay.

Once they reached the railroad terminus at Frisco, they planned to sell their mounts, board the Utah Southern to the Great Salt Lake, and then take the Utah Central to Ogden. Frisco was a little farther than Milford station, but because it was a rowdy mining camp and not a quiet cattle town, they figured they'd be less likely to be noticed there than at Milford station, where more cows boarded trains than humans.

Although Charlie had never been to the Frisco mining camp, he'd heard plenty of stories about it, and he relayed quite a few to Ophelia and Zeke during their journey. The stories entertained Ophelia but also increased her fear and anxiety. All she wanted to do was get home safely. She worried that, after all they'd been through, they'd get mixed up in some kind of trouble in Frisco and never make it home to Ogden.

The scowl on her brother's face told her he found Charlie and his stories more irritating than amusing. Even though she hadn't seen Ezekiel for a long time, she could still read him. She wanted him to like Charlie. But the more time the two men spent together, the more Charlie seemed to grate on Ezekiel's nerves.

On the grueling one-hundred-thirty-mile ride from Grafton to Frisco, a stream of worries trickled through her mind. She worried Luther would discover she was alive and find her. She worried that when they got home, Charlie or Ezekiel would search out Luther, kill him, and be hanged. She worried about the posse from Silver Reef. She worried about Indians and road agents. She worried about Zeke and Charlie fighting. She worried Zeke would fight in Frisco. And she worried her woman's time would come.

She tried to conjure the fond memories of her childhood in the desert, like outings to the emerald-colored swimming holes and rock pools. Beauty abounded: flashes of orange and red Indian paintbrush; bright cacti blossoms standing out against pale-green sage; towering rock walls higher than any man-made structure she'd ever seen.

There was a time when she knew every plant and bush—maybe not the Latin names, but common names and medicinal uses. Long ago, she could track animals and almost always catch something for dinner. She'd known when a storm was coming and could practically smell the direction of the nearest creek. Almost every day of her childhood, her hands had touched earth and animals, both wild and tame. It felt like a lifetime ago. Traveling through the red desert again brought back memories of her stolen youth.

Her mind flipped from fond to bad memories and fear of impending disaster. Besides the ever-present danger of Indians and road agents, the most immediate trouble was in Frisco. Her brother's long hair and the peculiar Oriental talismans he donned would surely make him a target for insults. Put an angry, scar-faced half-breed, half-dressed as a Celestial, in a rough mining camp, add whiskey, and you were guaranteed a fight. The scar, which marred an otherwise handsome face, was most likely the badge of a brawler. Maybe he'd come by it some other way, but it surely hadn't been an accident. The remnants of violence etched into Ezekiel's face pained her. She couldn't bear the thought of him suffering anymore. No matter how big, strong, and tough he looked, she had an urge to protect him and see him safely home.

As soon as they arrived in Frisco, she wanted to find a mercantile and procure him new clothing. She imagined him sitting in a barber's chair, relaxed with his eyes closed, getting a nice shave and haircut. With a little sprucing up, no one would recognize him as a half-breed. But how could she suggest those changes without insulting him? She only wanted him to blend in with everyone else in order to avoid trouble.

She knew better than to bring up Ezekiel's appearance around Charlie. The two men seemed to take immediate opposition to each other's directions and advice. At one point in their journey, the trail had split. After an irreconcilable argument as to which direction to go, Zeke and Charlie parted ways, leaving Ophelia to choose between them. Charlie's face registered betrayal when she chose to follow her brother. "He's blood," she'd said, trying to soften the sting.

Charlie had ridden off in the other direction. Twenty minutes later Ophelia was relieved to see he had swallowed his pride and followed them. The only thing the two men agreed on was the necessity of killing Luther. If Ophelia wasn't so dead set against it, she would've used it as a common thread to mend the fissure between them.

Spring in the desert meant creeks flowed with runoff, so it wasn't hard to find water for the horses. Heart-shaped cottonwood leaves, still green and vibrant, fluttered in the breeze. As they rode, grouse, rabbits, and mule deer scurried away and bounded through the scrub. In the distance, a group of bighorn sheep blended with the landscape and stood still as statues. Birds sang and chattered.

She remembered traveling the same route when she was barely seventeen, before the railroad and the buffalo slaughter, before telegraph poles and barbed wire. Much had changed. And much remained the same. She'd been broken then, in both body and spirit. Resigned to death, she'd lain in the soft hot sand; her only hope to be fully dead before the vultures and coyotes feasted on her flesh. Death had seemed a welcome respite from her agony.

She'd been certain she would die alone there. And after the scavengers ate her flesh, her bones would lie sun-bleached and scattered with the bones of all the other creatures that had perished and disintegrated under the scorching sun. She remembered letting go and being at peace with her inevitable death. Now she hoped that when she faced death again, she'd feel the same way. But back then, she'd had nothing to live for, so it'd been easy to let go. Now, she had her brother, Charlie, money, and hope for the future.

They reached the stage road out of Toquerville and continued north. After many miles, the orange sand, arroyos, and deep canyons of fiery red rocks covered with inky black stains gave way to firmer ground: hills covered with piñon pine, juniper trees, scrub oak, and high desert sage. Piney scents filled the late afternoon air. Fields of cheerful balsamroots spanned like a giant yellow carpet all the way to the white-tipped granite mountains. She'd mostly spent the last decade indoors, a night owl, engaged in activities she'd rather forget, and she was grateful for an opportunity to be outdoors, riding a horse and sleeping under the stars. Much had changed within her since the last time she'd traveled this land, but the spirited girl who loved horses, and hunting and swimming in rivers, was still there.

Although they had left the desert, sand still coated the rims of their canteens, stuck to their teeth and tongues, nested in every orifice, and clung to their clothes like a dusty aura. Ophelia pined for a creek to bathe in. Her brother rode ahead of her. Somewhere in him the boy was still there, and she longed to find him.

Charlie rode ahead of Zeke. He was a good man who could see past what she'd once been. Ophelia tried to imagine settling down for a life with him. She enjoyed his company. But she didn't want to marry, because she'd lose all rights to her money and property. A man who seemed like a perfect gentleman could easily turn into a tyrant after marriage. She'd known many women who thought they were escaping the horrors of prostitution only to end up with such men.

Thanks to the money and property Pearl had left her, she'd never again have to sell herself to a man in order to survive. And she still had the ruby necklace. Pearl had used it as collateral to get a loan for the house. Sometimes that necklace felt like a medal of honor and sometimes a mark of shame. She was fortunate, and she knew she should be content. But Luther's resurrection clouded her mind. How could she be happy and at peace when he had risen, and with him the nightmare of her youth?

As much as Ophelia tried to focus on happy things, dreadful images of Luther surged as strong and constant as the spring runoff. The more she tried to close the lid on those memories, the more sights and sounds and words and feelings she didn't care to remember came flooding back. She saw his dark shape in the doorway of their homestead the first day he arrived. She saw his hairy toe poking through a hole in his sock and heard the phllt-phllt sound of him sitting at the table day after day shuffling cards.

In the Old Testament, God had tested Job's faith by taking away everyone and everything he loved and leaving him impoverished and blind. If what happened to Ophelia in her youth had been a test from God, she'd failed. When God took away her parents and replaced them with Luther, she'd lost her faith in God. Only memories of her father and Ezekiel kept her from losing faith in men as well.

Feelings of gratefulness and love vied with hate and shame. She pictured her uncle, the charlatan, living as a Mormon, smiling, laughing, praying, and stuffing his face with Widow Hopkins's famous pie. He'd been "scouring the territory for her." Why? Did he know she was the one who had shot him? Did he still pine for the missing ruby necklace? What would he do if he found her? Would he be remorseful or vengeful?

She was taking her brother and Charlie home with her. But could either man ever settle down? Both had restless spirits. She had watched Charlie ride his bronco up rocky buttes and down steep bluffs as calmly as if the untrained beast were an extension of his own body. For nearly a decade, he had lived amongst outlaws, pretending to be one. He was more accustomed to sleeping on the ground under a blanket of stars than in a bed under a woolen blanket. And even though Charlie and Zeke had both sworn oaths, Ophelia doubted either man would easily give up the vendetta of defending her long-lost honor.

Three

While a thick slice of pink light still graced the western horizon, they stopped to make camp near a creek. Zeke hunted prairie chickens while Charlie watered the horses. Ophelia walked down to the creek, away from Charlie so she could wash in private. She undressed, spread her clothes on a rock, and waded into the cool water. She didn't mind the outdoor life, but her woman's time was approaching, and she preferred to be living indoors when it came. Although the air was still a little warm, the water was cold, so she washed quickly, before her feet and legs went numb. For a brief moment, all she wore was the ruby necklace. Soft evening sunlight glinted off the clear water.

Downstream, Charlie splashed water on his face while the horses gulped and snorted. Even at a distance, she felt the magnetism between them. He looked up, noticed her, smiled, and quickly turned his head when she caught his gaze. She smiled as she dried herself and put on clean undergarments. After she dressed, she hitched her skirt and walked barefoot with her boots tucked under her arm toward Charlie.

She stood at the edge of the creek with him, placed her boots on the bank, squeezed the water out of her hair, and twisted it in a knot. "Thanks for taking the horses, Charlie. I was in dire need of a wash."

"Hope you don't think I was spying. I didn't realize you were there until I looked up and saw you."

"I figured as much. You're too much of a gentleman to spy

on a woman bathing."

He smirked and looked away. A difficult question that had been on her mind slid off her tongue as naturally as the creek flowed. "Charlie, why on earth do you carry around that handbill with the outlaws' pictures on it? Are you still employed by the Pinkertons?"

He hesitated before he answered. "No, not officially. Anyway, it's hard to explain. Some men hunt gems and minerals, others hunt game. I hunt men. I can't help myself. When that doctor examined my skull, he said being a detective was my destiny."

He stopped speaking abruptly and looked at her. "I apologize. I just remembered that a doctor told you because of your hair and skull shape, you were destined to become a lady of convenience. You know all that skull stuff is probably a load of bull. Truth is, I started hunting criminals the day I went after the scoundrel who ruined my sister, and I've never been able to stop. As for those two outlaws on the handbill . . . well, quite honestly, the bounty is substantial, and I could really use it."

Ophelia sighed. "Charlie, I intend to compensate you handsomely for finding Ezekiel. If you don't want the ruby necklace as payment, I can pay you in gold or notes. Despite any feelings that might have developed between us, we have a business agreement, and I intend to make good on it. You have certainly gone above and beyond the call of duty, coming all the way out here with me."

He stood close and placed his hands on her shoulders. She felt the weight and warmth of them. The accumulation of each intimate gesture, and even the subtlest physical contact between them, heightened both her anxiety and her excitement. With him so close, her heart quickened, and the blood coursed through her veins faster. She breathed deeply and tried to appear at ease.

Charlie's bronco attempted to nuzzle his head between them.

Hot horse breath and a cadre of flies interrupted their intimate moment. Charlie shooed the horse away. The flies lingered. He held Ophelia by the shoulders again and addressed her as if she were a child. "The hardest part of this job, Ophelia, is taking your money. It doesn't feel right. I suppose this was always the danger of doing business with the fairer sex, especially one as fair as you." He stroked her cheek. The bronco had begun to wander off a little too far. Charlie whistled through his teeth and the horse turned around. The man had a way with beasts.

A gunshot rang out. Charlie drew his pistol, stepped away, and scanned all directions.

"Charlie, that's just Ezekiel hunting for dinner."

"I'm going to scout the area just in case. As long as I don't find any signs of danger, we'll stay here tonight."

Ophelia hobbled her horse and then gathered firewood. She still felt tingly and excited from her exchange with Charlie. The attraction between them had grown so strong, if not for Ezekiel's presence, their relationship might have taken an intimate turn.

Until Charlie had come along, she'd sworn she would never have intimate relations with a man again. But his tender ways and the fact that he'd found Ezekiel changed her mind. She could compensate him with money, gold, or the necklace, and certainly didn't need to repay him with her favors. And yet that's what he seemed to want. She wondered if his infatuation with her would last. She bent over, picked up a large piece of wood, and felt her back ache. Exhausted and saddle sore, all she wanted to do was eat, drink, and collapse into sleep.

Zeke was sitting on the ground plucking prairie chickens. She dropped the woodpile and sat next to him. He continued plucking the birds. This was the first they'd been together alone. She reached out to touch his long thick braid. He recoiled. She quickly drew her hand away. She held it in the air for a second and then rested it in her lap, sensing he didn't want her to touch him. He wore an irritated scowl. But she didn't give up. She grinned, made a silly face at him, and stuck out her tongue.

Despite himself, the scowl became a smile, and he shook his head at his younger sister in the same exasperated manner as he had when they were children. "Ophelia, can't you see I'm busy? Why don't you go start the fire?"

"You look more Indian now than you ever did when we were growing up, Zeke."

He eyed her and continued plucking in silence. He'd become a hardened man unaccustomed to touch, the type of man who bristled at a gentle hand, as if it were as dangerous as a knife. She studied his moccasins, chaps, Celestial-style shirt, and the vaquero hat he'd placed on the ground next to him. With a sudden, swift movement, he unsheathed his Bowie knife. She jumped.

He smiled a mix of amusement and insult. "What did you think? That this was for you?" He shook his head and sighed. "I'm starving. Make a fire so we can eat." With a few efficient cuts, he gutted each prairie chicken and then wiped his hands on a bush.

"You actually look like a curious mixture of Indian, Celestial, and vaquero all rolled into one."

He let out a loud sigh. "For Christ's sake, Ophelia, I didn't know this was a fashion parade." He stood up, did a double take of her boots, and aimed his bloodstained knife at them. "How can you possibly talk to me about fashion, when you're wearing those boots?"

She stared down at Red Farrell's old boots, and turned her feet from side to side, admiring them, surprised at how she'd forgotten about them, how they didn't seem peculiar to her anymore, or even filled with Red Farrell's ghost. "Full Wellingtons, embossed cuffs. They're damned good boots for riding."

She angled her legs to show them off better. "You like 'em?"

He stared at them. "Those are men's boots."

She nodded. "I know. I took them off a dead man. A man I killed; was forced to kill, because he was trying to steal Momma's necklace." The way she said *momma* sounded childish to her right after she said it, and she felt silly for a second. She took the ruby necklace from under the collar of her dress and fingered the gemstones. "I do believe he aimed to kill me in order to steal the necklace. So it wasn't murder. It was self-defense." She paused, awaiting his approval. He was silent. "You know, the way Uncle Luther, and then Red Farrell, came after this necklace, I reckon it must be worth a fortune."

Zeke's eyes were tired. "Must be," he said without enthusiasm. He cleaned his hands in the stream, dried the knife on his pants, sheathed it, returned to where Ophelia sat, and picked up the birds.

She stood up and gathered the woodpile. "Charlie says Red Farrell was a dangerous outlaw, wanted for all kinds of crimes. He would most definitely have killed me if I didn't kill him first. Ever hear of him? Red Farrell?"

Zeke paused for a couple of seconds, squinted back in memory, and shook his head no. "You don't have to justify your actions to me," he said.

"You ever have to kill someone, Zeke? It's a terrible thing, even when it has to be done."

Zeke looked her steadily in the eyes. "Ophelia, it'd be best if you didn't know too much about me and what I've been doing the past decade."

She nodded in agreement, looked at her boots, and swallowed her awkwardness. "Well, considering that, maybe it would be a good idea to change your look. Haircut, new clothes, new man, new life, what do you say?"

"What are you proposing?"

She would not be deterred by his hard, intense manner. He was, after all, her brother, and she aimed to keep him safe. "Short hair, a European-style suit, gold pocket watch, Prince Albert hat, maybe even spectacles." She looked at him, imagining it. "I bet no one would even know—" Realizing how insulting what she was about to say might sound to him, she stopped.

"Know what? That I'm a half-breed?"

"Sorry. It's just—you know how people are. I wish they weren't that way, but they are."

"Didn't I just kill these birds? What makes you think I need spectacles? I might wear a bowler or a porkpie, but I will never wear a topper. And I don't need spectacles." He shook his head and slung the birds over his shoulder. "Fine, Ophelia. I'll be your Indian dress-up doll if that'll make you happy. Truth is, I may have dropped a match back in Silver Reef, so it wouldn't hurt to change my look."

He was right; it was best she didn't know about his crimes. Their future looked bright. All they had to do was let go of the past. "It won't make me happy to change your looks. I don't care how you look. I like the Indian part of you. I just don't want any more trouble. I've had trouble all my life, and I can't take much more. If something happened to you, I couldn't go on living."

He snorted. "I'm past giving a damn what anyone thinks of me. But I don't want any more trouble either, Ophelia. I've had my fair share of it, and I'm tired, too. I'm not an Indian or a white man. And I'm certainly not a Celestial. I'm nothing, no one, and I don't belong anywhere."

"We were a family once, Zeke. We belonged together. We're still part of each other. We're blood. Mother loved you more than anything. And Pa loved you too—in his own way."

They walked through sage and willow grass to the place they'd left their bedrolls. Zeke stopped and looked at her. "Do you remember Zachery Mills from Independence? Hair as white as cotton, big buggy eyes, always getting a lickin' for playing pranks?"

"No, can't say I do."

"You were probably too young to remember. Anyway, he was forever coming by with some little thing for Pa to fix, because his own pa was off in the cavalry. His mother always sent him with a little gift in exchange for Pa's help. One time Pa replaced an ax handle for him, and when he handed it back to little Zachery Mills, he said, 'Here you go, son.' When Zachery left, Pa turned to me and said, 'Let's go to the house, boy. I bet dinner's ready.' He might as well have punched me in the stomach. All my life, I just wanted him to call me 'son.' He called Zachery Mills 'son,' and he called me 'boy.' "

"Just one word." Ophelia nodded, wishing their father could have said it.

"Just one word. I waited my whole life to hear it. Now it's too late. Do you know what it's like to be no man's son?"

They continued walking. Ophelia laughed. "I don't know what it's like to be no man's son. But I do know what it's like to be every man's girl."

Zeke stopped walking. He looked at her, shocked and serious. "Sweet Jesus, Ophelia! I'm sorry. What you went through makes me sick. None of it would have happened if I had stayed that night instead of riding off like a coward." He shook his head and couldn't seem to stop shaking it, like he could shake the whole thing from ever being true. "Goddamn it, I don't want to imagine. It makes me so mad. I want to kill someone." His eyes flamed with anger.

"Zeke, if you hadn't left Grafton that night, you wouldn't be standing here today, because they would have hanged you. Luther told them you were a traitor to Black Hawk. He told them that, and they believed it—"

"Yes, because Luther is a white man, and I'm a half-breed. Even though he'd only been in Grafton for a week, and I'd been there most of my life, they believed him over me."

Ophelia saw in his eyes how he seemed to be remembering something from back then, and she sensed there was something he wanted to say. But he didn't say it, and she didn't press him. He turned begging-dog-eyes toward her. It was a look she hadn't seen since they were children when he was pleading for her licorice stick.

"Please, please, Ophelia. Say I can kill Uncle Luther. It's my duty."

Ophelia shook her head. "Besides the fact that revenge killing is wrong, it's also a hanging offense. I couldn't live if that happened." She looked at him. He looked away. A brief moment of silence passed. "Besides that, do you realize Luther could be the only person left who knows who your real father was? Maybe your real father's still alive. You could be some man's son."

"And if Luther knows the truth about my father, why on earth would he ever tell it to me?"

Ophelia nodded in agreement. "That's true. All that ever came out of his mouth was horseshit."

"Don't fret, Ophelia. You can dress me up. I at least owe you that. Now let's get the fire lit and roast these birds. I'm starving."

Hungry as they were, all conversation stopped while they ate. They chewed the meat from the delicate bones of prairie chickens and mopped up beans with johnnycakes. After they were through eating, they leaned back on their saddlebags and Charlie passed a bottle of whiskey around. The sky was now dark, and the first stars twinkled. Ophelia wrapped a blanket around her shoulders and scooted closer to the fire.

Ezekiel took a swig from the liquor bottle, passed it back to Charlie, then stretched out, propped his head on his bag, and looked at the sky. "Ophelia, you remember when that disease killed our parents? I didn't know what to do. I was angry, but I didn't know how to get revenge on a disease, so I blamed God. Then I realized there was no sense in that. It was my job to protect you, and I failed. With Luther still alive, I have someone to blame. He's a disease in the form of a man. And I know how to kill a man. I wish you'd grant me permission to do what we all know needs doing."

It was the most he'd spoken in front of Charlie. Ophelia glanced across the fire at Charlie and then at Zeke. "What happened wasn't your fault. You were just a boy. He was supposed to protect us." She turned her head and waved a stream of smoke from her eyes. "What I have a hard time understanding is why Mother wrote to him in the first place."

"I don't believe he's our relation. He bears no resemblance to Mother. Why, there's more resemblance between us," said Zeke.

Ophelia wanted Luther to be a stranger and not a blood relation. It didn't feel right to hate her kin. But Zeke's premise didn't make sense. "How would he have known about us? And who could he possibly be, if not Mother's brother?" Ophelia shook her head. "Anyway, we must put it behind us. Nothing can be undone. We're together again. Let's move forward and be grateful for that. Maybe we should sell the house in Ogden and leave the Utah Territory so you won't be tempted to hunt him."

Ophelia sensed Ezekiel's restless and troubled spirit. She felt the burden of his guilt and wanted to put an arm around him. But she knew he'd be uncomfortable with the sign of affection, especially in front of Charlie. "Ezekiel, I killed Luther once, and I'll tell you it made no difference. I didn't feel any better. I only felt better because I didn't worry that he was searching for me. And you know I didn't have to become a whore. That's not your fault, either. I found work in a laundry, and I could have stayed there. It was horrible, but I wasn't starving. I chose to go to Ogden, take up with Pearl, and work at the parlor house. Honestly, it wasn't all terrible. Pearl protected me from the worst of it. And I became one of the wealthiest unmarried women in Ogden."

Charlie shook his head and corrected her. "Pearl didn't help you out of charity. You were her little gold mine."

Ophelia sighed. She was tired of having this argument with Charlie. If he preferred to think of her as a victim of Pearl's corruption rather than someone who chose her own fate, so be it. She stared at him. He waited for her usual response, but she wouldn't argue with him anymore.

"Well, my sister chose to take her own life," Charlie finally said and stared, transfixed by the flames and his memories. It broke her heart to see such a jovial man so melancholy, and she felt a sudden gush of affection toward him.

Ezekiel shot a perplexed squint across the fire at Charlie. He knew nothing about Charlie, except that he'd been a reviled Pinkerton detective, hated by the miners. He didn't know the deep sadness lurking behind Charlie's easy manner. What happened to Charlie's sister wasn't one of his entertaining yarns.

Ezekiel turned his attention back to Ophelia as if Charlie wasn't even there. Ophelia hoped someday the two men would come to know and like each other. Charlie's chin dropped to his chest and a soft snore filled the silence. He went to sleep fast and hard. She wondered if he'd die that way too.

Ezekiel coaxed her to see things his way. "Ophelia, Luther lives, and by all accounts, he lives a good life, posing as a Saint and living amongst them. Sweet Jesus, can't they see him for the devil he is?"

"Maybe he's changed somehow. I know you didn't like her, but Widow Hopkins was a decent woman. A decent and shrewd woman, surely she wouldn't have married him if she didn't see some good there. Anyhow, let's not beat a dead horse. I'm tired."

"Sadly, he's not dead," said Ezekiel. They smiled wryly at each other.

Ophelia stared into the dying embers, remembering how easily their Uncle Luther could change his manners and his voice to suit his audience. She also remembered the way Widow Hopkins had blushed and swooned when he had kissed her hand. "My only worry is that once Luther hears I'm alive and was in Grafton, he'll try and track me down."

Zeke perked up. "See? If he was dead, you'd have nothing to worry about."

Charlie woke up, nodded in agreement, and pointed at Zeke. "That's a good point. I like that idea."

Ophelia looked from man to man. "I'm glad you finally agree upon something, but I regret it is something I am dead set against."

Zeke looked at her. "I played his cards and drank his whiskey. I shouldn't have run off and left you alone with him. It's my duty to right the wrong."

Charlie's head dropped to his chest again. This time he snored loudly. They stared at him. Ophelia laughed, and shook her head, amazed he'd never been killed in his sleep.

"Good Lord, are we going to have to listen to that all night? You can probably hear him in California," said Zeke.

Ophelia gently guided Charlie to a lying position on his bedroll and covered him with a blanket. The snoring was so loud it drowned out all the other night sounds and would have revealed their location to anyone passing in a ten-mile radius.

Four

After four long days of riding and three nights sleeping in the dirt under the stars, the travelers began to see clapboard shacks and shanties, marking the outskirts of Frisco.

Charlie stopped riding and looked behind him. He scanned the area, chewed his mustache, and then let forth an explosion of expletives. "Shit! Damn it! Oh, holy hell! That couldn't have been the last spring we passed. We forgot to fill up our canteens!" He took his hat off and squeezed it in his hands so hard it would have died if it'd been breathing.

Ophelia tried not to giggle. For days, Charlie had been stressing the importance of filling up on water before they arrived in Frisco. His tirade of curses tapered off into a whisper. He turned to Zeke and Ophelia. "How much water do you all have?"

Ophelia shook her canteen and grimaced. "Not much."

"About half," said Zeke.

"Damn it," said Charlie.

Ophelia had rarely seen him this flustered. "Charlie, there's a town, isn't there? Surely, we're not going to die of thirst," she said.

"No, we won't die of thirst, but it's not likely we'll be able to stay sober. There's more whiskey than water in Frisco. Plenty of zinc, copper, lead, silver, and even a little gold, but you can't drink any of that."

They rode until they came upon a cemetery. Beyond the cemetery was a steep wagon road leading to Frisco and the mining camp beyond. The train tracks ascended a gulley up the hill toward the mine shaft. To the north, clouds of smoke arose from giant beehive-shaped kilns built on the hillside. The cemetery was rather large, considering the town hadn't been there very long. Like other cemeteries in rough frontier towns, it had a densely populated boot-hill section. The section for babies and children had a lot of nice markers, but didn't take up too much space. Boot Hill, where rock piles marked the graves of men who'd died by violence, took up the most space, and scattered piles of rocks outnumbered the small cluster of nice headstones over where the respectable people had been buried.

Next to the cemetery gate, a cart piled with corpses surrounded by flies emitted a stench so strong, Ophelia covered her nose. Charlie squinted at the dead bodies rotting in the sun, frowned in disgust, and coughed. Voices drifted from the shade of a juniper tree where two gravediggers passed a bottle of spirits, seemingly oblivious to the slow decomposition of their charges. Neither the smell nor the flies instilled a sense of urgency within them. Ophelia, Zeke, and Charlie watched with varying degrees of revulsion. They stared at the men and awaited an explanation. None came.

"Hello there," Charlie finally called. "Was there some kind of mining accident?"

Heat waves shimmered, hovering just above the sandy earth. From the dappled shade of the juniper, one of the gravediggers squinted up at Charlie. The other man had stripped down to his union suit and was busy picking something from the sole of his bare foot. His dirty, sweat-stained clothes were splayed out on a sagebrush. He continually interrupted his foot picking to mop the perspiration from his forehead with a faded blue bandana. Ophelia figured if he produced that much perspiration just sitting in the shade sipping whiskey and picking at his foot, he'd fill a whole bucket once he actually picked up a shovel.

"Mining accident?" The man chuckled. "No. No mining accident. Six of these men the new marshal from Pioche kilt. See, he doesn't believe in jail. Troublemakers got two choices with him: they can either leave town; or stay forever in this underground hotel we're building. Besides the men the marshal kilt, about four of the others kilt each other. And there's probably about five we never got around to burying yesterday. Those are the stanky ones." He wiped his brow again and reached impatiently for the bottle.

His fellow gravedigger took a long swig before he passed the bottle, then shaded his eyes with his hand and looked up at them. When he saw Ophelia, his interest sparked, and he craned his neck to get a better look at her. "Let's have a look at you, miss," he called. "Don't hide back there! Come say hello to us boys. Give us a taste of yer quality. Did you bring her here to keep us company?" he asked Charlie.

Charlie glared at the man, rested his hand on his Colt, and said, "No, I did not. She's my wife, and you better stop gawking, or else your partner will have another body to bury."

With effort, the man pushed himself up to standing. He swayed like a branch in a breeze, though there wasn't much of a breeze. The horses flicked their tails at the swarming flies. Beads of sweat rolled down Ophelia's temple and the small of her back. She shooed flies from her face and wished they hadn't stopped to chat with the vile gravediggers.

The gravedigger in the union suit slurred and sputtered. "I'll gawk at whatever or whoever I damn well please. Ain't no crime in looking at a purdy lady. No harm in looking! Don't you try and take one of the only pleasures I got left. You self-righteous toffy-headed twat protector. Take that dandy pearl-handled Colt you got yer hand on, and shove it up—"

Ophelia rode forward and positioned her horse between the

man and Charlie's mount. "All right, Charlie, I've been gawked at before. Let's move on. I don't want trouble, and that stench is overwhelming." She stared at Charlie, shook her head, and spoke softer. "They're just clowns in the burial ground. Pay them no mind."

They turned their horses and rode away. Ophelia felt something terrible was going to happen. They hadn't even arrived in town yet, and they'd almost had a fight. "Stop!" she called to Zeke, who rode a ways ahead of her.

Charlie caught up from behind and halted. Ophelia addressed them both sternly. "Did you see those bodies? We need to keep our heads down and stay out of trouble. Charlie, don't pick a fight over a man gawking at me or insulting me. I worked in a brothel for nearly ten years, remember? I can handle drunks and insults."

He frowned. "I'm trying to forget, Ophelia. But you happen to remind me every chance you get. Besides, you worked at a parlor house not a brothel. There's a difference." He pulled out the handbill, studied the faces, and squinted back over his shoulder where the men still loafed.

Ophelia shook her head. "Charlie, the men on that paper bear no resemblance to those men. And even if they did, why get involved? Let's just stay out of trouble, so we don't join those unfortunate souls with reservations at the underground hotel."

They continued riding toward Frisco. Ophelia had grown attached to her spotted pony and didn't look forward to selling it at the livery. It had been a long time since she'd spent so much time on a horse, and the sweet spotted pony was good-natured, strong, and reliable. At the same time, her backside ached, and she looked forward to the comfort of rail travel. She wanted a warm bath, a hot meal, and a real bed.

They found a livery at the top of the hill near the railway station. After Charlie haggled with the liveryman, he turned to Ophelia and declared, "Well done, miss. Your strength and fortitude impress me. I've never in my life seen a member of the fairer sex spend that much time in a saddle without complaint."

Now that the pony was gone, Ophelia realized the pungent odor she'd attributed to him was actually coming from her. If Charlie got a good whiff of her, he might not declare her so fair. When she was seven years old, she had walked most of the Overland Trail with very little to eat. Nothing since, not even her near-death ordeal in the desert, had challenged her strength and fortitude as much as that journey.

She wanted to tell Charlie that the fairer sex wasn't so fair. They bled every month, bore children, and suckled infants, even when they had little to eat themselves. Society had created the concept of a lady. On the frontier and in factories, women didn't have the luxury of being ladies. Any observer of savages could plainly see that women in natural habitats were by no means fair of temper or physicality. But Charlie meant his remark as a compliment, and that was all that really mattered, so she smiled and held her tongue.

After they left the livery, they walked, laden with saddlebags on shaky legs, to the station. Charlie hadn't been able to get a high-enough price for his favorite saddle, so he carried it on his shoulder. The station agent watched from behind the counter as Ophelia and Charlie tried to make sense of the schedule. Time was not yet standardized, so train timetables were confusing and unreliable. Charlie moved his index finger across a row of tiny numbers and tried to find the arrival and departure time for the next train.

The station agent finally offered assistance. "This here's the terminus—end of the line. Train only comes once a day. Came 'bout an hour ago. So you've missed it."

Their bodies deflated in disappointment. They were tired of

traveling. Ophelia walked toward Zeke, who stood at the end of the platform and stared at the place where the track disappeared over the horizon. She cupped her hand to her mouth and yelled, "Just missed it. Next train doesn't come until tomorrow!" He nodded in resignation. She walked back to Charlie.

"Damn, just missed it," Charlie said under his breath and shook his head. He caught sight of a wanted poster nailed to the wall. The pictures were of the same men as on the handbill he carried in his pocket. He chewed his mustache while he stared at the poster with narrow, calculating eyes.

Ophelia reached up and gently removed the side of his mustache from his mouth. "Maybe castor oil will break this habit. It works for thumb-sucking babies," she teased.

The station agent also watched Charlie. The station was empty, and the agent didn't seem to have anything to do. Ophelia wished Charlie would give up both chewing his mustache and his obsession with outlaws.

"You some sort of detective? A Pinkerton maybe?" the agent asked.

Charlie turned, crestfallen and puzzled. "I was. Not anymore. How did you figure it?"

Ophelia sighed. It seemed obvious to everyone but him.

"It's in the way you were looking at that poster."

Charlie nodded. "You're very perceptive. Have the makings for a detective yourself."

The watchful agent took that as a compliment and began talking to Charlie as if he were a trusted acquaintance. "I spend a lot of time watching people. I've been instructed to keep an eye out for suspicious types, so it's part of my job. The train that leaves here every day is mixed freight loaded with silver. It could very well be a target for a robbery. I'm also looking for anarchists. They're big trouble—don't even care about making away with the loot. They'd blow up the train and all the loot with it, just to spread anarchy."

Charlie looked at the station agent, raised his brows, and cocked his head. "Yep, those anarchists are nothing but trouble. But the mining companies sure do take advantage. If they'd make a few concessions, the anarchists might not exist. But let's get back to these two." Charlie pointed at the poster. "That's some bounty. Have they been seen in the area?"

"Don't know about that. But there's armed guards on all the trains, so you don't need to worry."

Charlie patted his gun and grinned. "Oh, I'm not worried. If they hold up a train I'm on, they'll quickly realize they picked the wrong train."

Ophelia rolled her eyes. The station agent nodded toward her and Zeke. "Are those two ruffians your prisoners?"

She looked down at her dusty clothes and realized how dirty and disheveled she looked. "Excuse me, sir," she said to the agent. "I can hear you. I'm standing right here."

Charlie turned toward Ophelia. He reached deep inside his pocket, walked over, and offered her a handkerchief, which was miraculously clean. She wiped her face with it. Although it was clean, it smelled like him. She didn't mind the smell and felt a strange closeness to him because of it. She wiped the dust off her face and shook her head. Her eyes burned with indignation and embarrassment, not only about her outward appearance, but also because of the repugnant smell she recognized as herself. While she didn't mind Charlie's smell, her own was too much, and she desperately wanted a bath.

Charlie addressed the station agent. "No, these are certainly not prisoners. I wouldn't be so careless with prisoners, especially the Indian. This is Miss Ophelia Oatman. That man over there is her brother, Ezekiel Oatman."

Zeke had walked away when he heard they'd missed the train. He stood with his bag at his side and his arms crossed, waiting for them at the end of the platform. The station agent cast a curious glance toward him and then studied Ophelia closer.

"Oh, I apologize, miss. You were so covered with dust, and why with those er—trousers, I thought—well, I see now I was wrong. Please forgive my rudeness."

Ophelia looked down at her split riding skirt, surprised he could tell it wasn't a proper skirt. She narrowed her eyes at him. "Never mind, sir. I understand your error. Can you recommend a good hotel with baths? We have been riding almost four days, and obviously I must freshen up if I'm being mistaken for some sort of barbarian."

"A real bath's going to be difficult. Not much spare water around here, at least not potable water. The bath water tends to be on the murky side. Let's see . . ." He stroked his beard. "There's the San Francisco Hotel, but that's probably full. Otherwise, right across from it is the Sand Friend Sicko Inn, which is clean, but I have to warn you, it's run by Celestials."

Charlie and Ophelia exchanged glances. "Excuse me, sir, did you say the Sand Friend Sicko Inn?" asked Ophelia.

"Yes, it's an unfortunate name, but from what I hear it's clean and they have baths. All the other lodging houses . . ." he looked at Charlie knowingly. "Let's just say they're even less respectable than the one run by Celestials."

"Is the Sand Friend Sicko Inn likely to be full as well? Who lodges there?" asked Ophelia.

"Probably not. But it's popular with foreigners, folks who don't speak or read much English and aren't put off by the sign or the owners."

Charlie grinned. "That reminds me. A funny thing happened when I was in San Francisco once—"

"Charlie!" Ophelia glared at him and made a motion with her head that they should take leave of the station agent and not waste any more time. She was dying for a bath.

As the station agent predicted, the San Francisco Hotel was full. They crossed the street and stood in front of the Sand Friend Sicko Inn. Ophelia stared at the odd handwritten, misspelled sign nailed to the front door. The *d* in sand was backward. She heaved a deep sigh and hoped for the best. Besides the kilns, nothing in the whole town was made entirely of stone. Most of the dwellings were clapboard shacks with false fronts. The San Francisco Hotel was by far the sturdiest building and looked like it might actually have wood floors. The Sand Friend Sicko Inn didn't look so good, but there were no other choices.

Charlie spoke to the Celestial innkeeper, who nodded a lot, but clearly didn't understand a word he was saying. The innkeeper made an unintelligible response. Charlie spoke slower and very loud.

Ezekiel put his hand up, and shook his head. "He's not deaf. But we all will be if you continue shouting." He stepped forward and began to speak to the man in his own language. A bright smile of surprise flashed across the innkeeper's face. He came to life, smiling, talking, nodding, and laughing as he spoke with Ezekiel. As Ophelia witnessed the interaction between them, her heart swelled with a sudden love for the people who had accepted her half-brother. His almost hairless face and his long black braid were not so different from theirs. She beamed at Charlie. He looked confused and possibly upstaged.

Ezekiel turned to Ophelia, "How many rooms?"

She held up two fingers. Charlie said, "I don't need a room. I can sleep under the stars like we've been doing. It doesn't bother me."

"I'd feel better if you slept in a room. Can you two manage sharing a room without shooting each other, or do we need three?"

The men looked at each other and nodded in agreement. The

innkeeper gave Ezekiel the keys, who then handed one to Ophelia and one to Charlie. "Sorry O, the bath won't be ready for about an hour."

"It'll have to do." Ophelia studied Zeke. "Never mind me. Let's go find you new clothes and a barber. Charlie, we'll meet you back here later. You look tired. Go take a nap. Whatever you do, just please—stay out of the saloons."

Unwashed men covered with dirt and soot roamed the mining camp. Ophelia had fooled herself into thinking she didn't care what people thought about her. But for the past decade she'd hidden her shame behind expensive dresses and immaculate grooming. The parlor house girls and other whores believed that by dressing up and being clean on the outside, they wouldn't feel as dirty on the inside. Their strategy had been somewhat effective, as people tended to judge others by their appearance.

In her filthy, disheveled state, Ophelia felt a shame she hadn't experienced since she was a grubby young girl with nits in her hair. Although she had no desire to attract men, now that they were in a town surrounded by people, she was embarrassed by her smell and appearance. She wanted to transform Ezekiel into a respectable-looking man to protect him and keep him out of trouble, not because of vanity or propriety. His exotic look was bound to court trouble.

They walked past unstable dwellings clinging to the steep sandy earth. Women washed dishes in the open air; men threw dice; children played marbles in the dirt. A bottle tossed from a rowdy establishment on the hillside landed at their feet. Ezekiel stared at the bottle and then glared at the crowd of drunks and tried to determine the thrower. Smoke carried scents of grilled meat, and garbled male voices, punctuated by an occasional shrill cackle, filled the air.

The smell made Ophelia hungry. She looked at the bottle,

the oblivious drunks, and then Zeke. "Ignore it," she said and kept walking. Rough-looking, unwashed men stared openly and lewdly at her, despite her filthy appearance.

Down the hill toward the main road, a mercantile with a shade awning stood between a saloon and brothel. A woman lay on a bench, passed out and with limp limbs hanging over the sides; her neck bright pink with sunburn, and an empty whiskey bottle in the dirt just inches from her curled fingers. Ophelia fought an instinct to help her. If one of the parlor house girls had been found in that condition, she would have suffered Pearl's wrath and been thrown onto the street. Ophelia would help a girl once and give her a warning. But after the bottle or opium took a hold, it was usually too late.

The covered mercantile was a refuge from the heat and relentless sun. A good-natured proprietress showed them to the back of the store where four trunks full of men's clothes stood. Most of the clothing looked fairly well used. Ophelia wondered if the clothes had belonged to the naked dead men they'd seen in the cart. Ezekiel rummaged through the trunk, either oblivious to the possibility the clothing came from the dead, or just not caring, so Ophelia didn't mention it. He found a jacket, trousers, and a shirt with two missing buttons that fitted him. The mercantile proprietress said she'd mend the shirt while they waited. While they were looking at hats, Ophelia noticed a barber outside setting up a makeshift shop on the veranda. His setup was crude, but the timing was amazing.

"I think we're in luck, Ezekiel. Look at that. You can get your hair cut while she sews the buttons." The barber sat on a stool and spat a wad of tobacco, which landed in a pile at the edge of the veranda. "Is he the only barber in Frisco?" Ophelia asked the woman.

She stared out the open door and regarded the barber with irritation and revulsion. " 'Fraid so."

Ophelia walked outside and asked him how much he would charge to cut Ezekiel's hair. He looked at Zeke, noticed the long black braid, and spat again. "The only thing I'm a-gonna cut on that savage is his neck," he yelled.

Ezekiel and the woman heard his remarks through the opened door. The woman stood, grabbed a broom from behind the counter, came outside, and shook it at him. "You rude old coot, I'll cut *your* neck before the sun goes down if you don't start paying some rent for our shade. And I've told you a hundred times to stop spitting tobacco on the floor. Now clean it up!" She shook the broom at him one more time, leaned it against the wall, and walked back into the mercantile. He snarled and made threatening gestures with his razor at her back.

Ezekiel stood inside the mercantile doorway, unmoving yet watchful, like a predator before a strike. Ophelia spoke softly to the barber and convinced him to rent her his scissors, razor, and chair. She slid him some coins and shooed him toward the saloon.

Ophelia had often cut hair on Sundays at the Doll House: women's, men's, and sometimes even children's. People paid, traded, or did her favors to compensate. It felt more like penance than work, and she secretly enjoyed it. Confident she could cut her brother's hair better than the vile, tobacco-spitting barber, she coaxed Zeke outside and sat him in the chair. He sighed, closed his eyes, and, like Sampson, sacrificed his locks to the blade.

Two men passing by stopped and gawked. Ophelia wished they'd get on with their business. She saw, too late, that the barber's sign advertising haircuts was still propped against the mercantile post. Two more men saw the sign, stopped, watched, and waited, presumably for haircuts.

In Frisco, like most other mining towns, there were nine men to every woman. Even though she was covered in dust and wearing a split riding skirt, men still stared at her like hungry dogs drooling over a side of beef. The sun was just about to disappear beyond a distant hill, yet most able-bodied men were still working the mine. The men who waited for haircuts were a ragtag, lame, scraggly bunch. Nevertheless, she found them menacing and threatening, like they'd just crawled from shallow graves in the cemetery. In fact, it wouldn't surprise her if the careless gravediggers occasionally buried the living. Despite the vile appearance of the men waiting for her service, it touched her that they'd spend what little they had on a haircut from her rather than ardent spirits.

She did her best to ignore their lecherous stares and concentrate on cutting Ezekiel's thick raven locks, which were laden with dust and grease. Her fear of the men made her feel like a fraud. She'd talked such a tough game about her years as a whore. In truth, she'd mostly been a spoiled courtesan and a madam's assistant, whose main customers were wealthy and well-bred. She trembled and fought to steady the scissors.

In the chair with his eyes closed, Ezekiel seemed blissfully unaware of the men gathered and waiting.

Ophelia's hand holding the scissors shook so much, she could barely steady it. With a length of Ezekiel's hair in the comb, she froze and accidently tugged it.

His eyes snapped opened. "Are you almost done?" He squinted at the line of men and chuckled. "Looks like you got a few more customers after me."

She tried to compose herself. The men had lined up for haircuts, not fornication. Perhaps all they desired was a soft touch in a hard world; a woman's hand on their shoulder; her fingers running through their hair and her bosom near their face. Even in her pungent, disheveled state, she'd be an improvement over the cantankerous barber who served the camp. But there were too many. Too many men.

And then she remembered Christmas Eve at Johnny's farm. There'd been a big dinner and heavy drinking late into the night. People were slumped in chairs and passed out on the floor. Ophelia had escaped the party and curled up on a vacant bed in a quiet corner of the house she thought no one knew about. She awoke to hands groping her and tearing at her dress. How many were there? She couldn't remember exactly, didn't want to; too many, too many men. She screamed for help and they gagged her. It was Christmas, and that made it more terrible. She wasn't even working.

When Pearl found out the next day, she called for blood. But it was Christmas. There'd been a fight the previous Christmas that had ended in death, and no one wanted that again. So she was paid, and money was supposed to make it all right. That was the last time either of them went to Johnny's place for Christmas—or any other time. And it was the beginning of the end of Pearl and Johnny.

Ophelia looked at the pack of men lined up for haircuts—too many men. A pack of men were like rabid dogs that came for you when you slept and turned your dreams into nightmares. She couldn't steady her hand.

Zeke stared at the shaking scissors next to his scarred cheek. He looked again at the line of rough men, studied Ophelia, and seemed to understand her predicament. He carefully pried the scissors from her hand and brushed the loose hairs from his head and shoulders. "Thank you, O. I feel lighter without all that hair."

Unable to meet his gaze, she stared at the long obsidian locks lying in the dirt. A breeze lifted a few dark strands and carried them away in a swirl of air and dust. They were little bits of his soul that would never be recovered, and Ophelia already regretted the haircut she had given him that had erased his Indian half.

She picked her bonnet off the ground and stared at the stray strands of his hair clinging to it. Her own hair had escaped its tight bun and hung past her shoulders in a messy tangle held in place with dust and sweat. Her hair had attracted the men. She cursed it. She cursed the ruby necklace. And she cursed her lustful nature that drove her back into the arms of a man even though she knew doing so would end in heartbreak and disaster.

"Ezekiel, cut my hair."

"What?"

"Cut my hair." She nodded at the scissors. "Do it. Cut it all off."

"Why?"

"I shouldn't have cut your hair."

"Don't worry, Delilah. I'm not Samson; my hair will grow back. Ignore those men. Leave them for the barber." He guided her by the elbow away from the pack of waiting men.

One of them shouted. "Hey! Where do you think you're going with the barberess? I've been waiting for that fine specimen to cut my hair."

The next man in line, whose white, shoulder-length hair poked out from under a tattered hat, scowled at Ezekiel. "You can't just walk off with her." He took a few menacing steps toward them.

The old man wouldn't have been intimidating if it weren't for the angry crowd behind him. Zeke stood between Ophelia and the men. He straightened to his full height, took a step toward the old man, and towered over him. The man took two steps back and looked behind him for support from his ragtag army. Ophelia's fears were about to be realized. She imagined Zeke's body piled on the cart with the other corpses at the bottom of Boot Hill.

The rich perfumed stench of cigar smoke filled the air, and Charlie strolled toward them with a fat, smoldering stogie hanging from his mouth. The brothel door opened and a woman tossed piss from a chamber pot onto the road. She shielded her eyes from the last bright rays of sinking sun with her hand, squinted at the group of scraggly men, and retreated into the brothel. The scent of steaming urine wafted toward them. The piss stench mixed with the cigar fumes, and turned Ophelia's stomach, which was already knotted with fear.

Charlie watched the tension build as Zeke and the old man glared at each other. "What kind of trouble has that Injun stirred up now?" he whispered to Ophelia.

She glared at him.

"I'm joking," he said and tipped the ash from his cigar.

"They saw me cutting his hair. Now they all want haircuts."

Charlie shook his head and laughed.

Panic-stricken, Ophelia looked at him like he was crazy. "This is serious."

He stopped laughing and walked calmly over to Ezekiel and the old man.

"Excuse me!" He addressed the whole group of men in a loud, confident tone. "Sir, sirs, you should all be fairly warned before you employ this lady to cut your hair." With a hand motion, he beckoned Ophelia forward. She took a few steps toward him. He pulled her to him, put his hand on her shoulder, and regarded her with pity. "This poor woman has palsy. She can cut hair real fine until she starts to shake. A few men have been cut real bad. One almost lost his ear."

Ezekiel retreated a few steps, listened to Charlie, and tried to suppress a grin. Ophelia couldn't believe how fast Charlie could concoct such a story. What would stop him from lying to her? Was she a fool to trust him?

A general rumble rose from the men. Their heads shook with disappointment; most wandered away. The old man with white scraggly hair stood his ground, squinted at Charlie, and scrutinized Ophelia. She exaggerated the tremor of fear already coursing through her body until she shook. And then she jerked her head to the side twice, silently praying she wasn't overdoing it. The old man looked at the ground.

"Tell you what." Charlie addressed him and the few others who remained. "Anyone who's been waiting for a haircut can have a drink on me. But she's my girl, and she won't cut hair today because I don't want to be responsible for all the cut-up ears." He gestured to the saloon between the mercantile and the brothel. "Go on in there, wet your whistles, and I'll pick up the tab."

"I have a question," shouted a sinewy man wearing a dusty, torn shirt. "Is she available for activities other than haircutting, which don't involve blades, where a few palsy jerks may actually enhance the experience?"

Ribald laughter filled the air. Charlie stood upright, his body tensed, and his hand went to his holster. The crowd of men stepped back. A few men made uncoordinated motions to find their guns.

"Charlie," Ophelia pleaded in a loud whisper, trying to reel him back to his senses.

He took his hand from where it hovered over his holster, crossed his arms, and tucked his hands under his armpits. "Absolutely not! She is my wife. And if anyone insults her again, they'll be meeting me for a duel."

Ophelia wished he'd stop saying she was his wife.

"If she's so shaky, how come that Injun lets her cut his hair?" asked the white-haired man.

"Well, you saw him, didn't you?" Charlie mimed a cut across his cheek. "He's cut up already, so it makes no difference." He sighed, relit his cigar, took a big inhale, let it out, and looked at the sky. "Now I'm getting tired of this. I don't owe you any explanations, and I don't owe you a drink, but I offered you all one anyway. And my hospitality is about to expire because this jabbering has given me a headache."

Charlie and Ophelia walked to the mercantile doorway and stood together. The crowd broke and the men shuffled into the saloon. As they were filing in, the barber came out. He turned and bellowed to their backs. "Get yer cut and shave! Two-cent special today only!" They ignored him and continued into the saloon as if he didn't exist.

"You got a customer," Charlie said to the barber and pointed at the chair where the old white-haired man sat, eyes closed; his lips moving as if in prayer.

Zeke emerged from the mercantile wearing a stylish hat and the new clothes draped over his arm. Charlie watched the last of the men go into the saloon. He grinned. "Looks like I got some drinks to buy. Good thing the whiskey isn't as dear as the water."

Ophelia offered Charlie a pouch of bullion. "This is for the drinks. Good Lord, Charlie, I've never seen a more accomplished fibber. You deserve an award for that."

He pushed the pouch back toward her and inspected Zeke. "Let's see your hair."

Zeke removed his hat.

Charlie nodded his approval. "Very nice."

Zeke patted his head. His hand reached for the braid that wasn't there. "Are my ears still there?"

Five

The innkeeper spoke to Ezekiel in a language that sounded like wind chimes in a violent storm. Ezekiel turned to Ophelia and translated. "Your bath is ready and waiting."

Relieved and anxious to bathe, Ophelia climbed the warped stairs to her room. A corrugated iron horse trough filled with warm, murky water waited in the middle of the room. The water-stained floorboards looked thin, and she imagined the tub breaking through the floor while she was in it. She almost dragged it away from the rotten wood, but it was heavy and she was tired. A clean but discolored towel hung on a plain wooden chair next to the makeshift tub. With shaky hands, she undressed, then eased into the narrow tub, wishing she had a drink to settle her nerves. The water was still warm but smelled sulfurous, and although undrinkable, she supposed it was fine for a bath.

Ophelia tried to bury the memory of that horrible Christmas at Johnny's. Soon after that day, Pearl had fallen ill, and all of Ophelia's time had gone to nursing her and then grieving when she died. Somehow the pack of men waiting for haircuts had unearthed the buried memory. She soaked until the water turned cool, vowing never to think of that day again. While drying herself, she sniffed her skin and realized that she'd replaced her body odor with a sulfurous smell so strong, it couldn't be masked with perfume or soap.

She dressed quickly and knocked on Ezekiel's door. Despite

her guilt about cutting his Indian hair, she was eager to see how he looked. He peered out, saw her, and opened the door. She walked in, shut the door, and flopped on the bed without taking her boots off, figuring neither Ezekiel nor Charlie would care anyway.

Ezekiel's suit was untouched and draped over a worn chair in the corner. "Well," she said and gestured to the suit. "It's not going to bite you. Try it on."

Zeke turned his back to her, took off his old shirt, and brushed some stray hairs from his neck. Shirtless, with his hands on his hips, he faced the new clothes.

Ophelia watched her brother with concern. "I'm sorry, Ezekiel. You don't have to change the way you look. You're fine the way you are." She closed her eyes and sighed. "I just thought—"

"Ophelia, hush. You're right. It's time for me to get a fresh start. I don't like the person I've been for the last ten years. And if the law catches up to me, or someone recognizes me— Anyway, this is for the best." He nodded at the suit.

Forgetting modesty, he turned toward her. His muscled hairless chest was riddled with faded scars. Ophelia stared, unable to look away. She joked to hide her horror. "Looks like you've been wrestling with bears."

He expelled a long, loud sigh before he spoke. "I've had to fight to survive. But I'm ready to be someone new. Same as you, I suppose. You're a different person now. I'm sure you dress differently too." He eyed his new clothes with skepticism and felt for his missing hair. "You change your attire and then you start to feel different. Is that how it works?"

Ophelia pondered his question as she stared at her boots. She remembered removing them from Red Farrell's lifeless feet. When she'd first pulled his boots on, she'd felt like him, like his spirit was inside her. It was a curious feeling she knew better than to talk about—even with Zeke. She moved her ankles from side to side and watched the boots' metronomic movement. Why did she still wear them? So many times she'd meant to get rid of them, yet somehow they ended up on her feet again.

Zeke watched her. "I think it's time for you and those boots to part ways."

"Yes, you're right. They're a living reminder of my unfortunate past, and all the ugly things I had to do in the name of survival."

"Except they're not living; they're boots." Zeke grinned at her as if she were a lunatic, then turned his attention back to the waiting clothes."

"Please don't feel obligated to change your clothes on my account."

"I'm going to do it. It's just—maybe I should have a bath first."

"There's still a tub of water in my room, but I warn you, it has an extremely sulfurous odor, which seems to be coming from me now." She sniffed her arm again. "You could take a cat bath." She nodded toward the basin and towel on a table in the corner. "Don't worry. When we get to my house in Ogden, you can take a long hot bath with clean water."

He poured some water into the washbasin. It came out thick and brown.

"I'm dying of thirst," said Ophelia. "But I'm not drinking that water."

Zeke washed himself. The water ran in reddish-brown rust streaks down his neck. It combined with the dirt from his body to produce a deep brownish sludge in the basin. He dried himself and began to dress, handling the clothes as if they were made of delicate paper.

Ophelia couldn't help but watch. She'd seen enough male bodies to recognize his was mighty strong and handsome, despite the scars. While the bodily scars could be covered, nothing could hide the unfortunate scar that marred his face. He was a mix of two races, and the best of both made up his features: high cheekbones a slightly flared yet aquiline nose, exotic brown eyes rimmed with the faintest blue. He had one of the most handsome and stately countenances she'd seen on any man except for maybe his former employer, Mr. Gee. Perhaps that's what had bound them: the mixed race and the resulting burden of exotic male beauty, which they both possessed and white men probably couldn't bear. Maybe Zeke's handsome face had incited violence because men were jealous. Maybe they even lusted after his beauty. She knew too well that repressed desires often manifested themselves through cruelty and brutality.

Anyway, damn that scar, and damn the person who gave it to him, whoever he was. The scar was obviously from a knife and not from claws. That was all she knew, and most likely all she'd ever know, because she couldn't bring herself to ask him the details. When the time came, maybe he'd tell her.

The crisp new shirt was made whiter against Zeke's copper skin. It fit perfectly. Zeke cocked his head to both sides and sat on the edge of the bed without buttoning it all the way up. "Feels funny. A little stiff."

"That's to be expected with new clothes. They soften once you put them on and move about."

Ophelia had unbuttoned the top three buttons of her dress, exposing the ruby necklace. Zeke reached over and inspected the gems. "I can't believe Ma had a necklace like this." He studied her boots again. "Ha! The red rubies match the embossed cuffs. Is that why you wear them boots? Because they match the necklace?"

Ophelia chuckled. "Maybe that's why Red Farrell wanted the necklace—to wear with his boots! Maybe he was one of them types who like putting on ladies' clothes and undergarments."

Zeke stood and finished buttoning his shirt. When he reached the last button, he grimaced. “Neck’s a little tight.”

“Don’t worry. This is temporary. When we get to Ogden, I’ll have a tailor make a suit that fits you like a second skin.”

He stared at his old buckskin pants and chemise shirt clumped on the chair. “I don’t believe a suit will ever feel like skin for me, Ophelia. I’ll keep my old clothes to wear when I’m not in public.” He put the necklace with the strange Oriental talisman around his neck and hid it under his shirt. “We may hide our secrets, but they’re always with us,” he said as he tucked his shirt in. Then he put the vest on and slid into the jacket.

“Very handsome,” said Ophelia.

He put the hat on and looked around for a mirror, but there was none. “Dressing like a dandy has sure caused me to work up a thirst. I’m going to get a drink.” He patted the empty pockets of his new suit and rummaged through the pockets of his old clothes for coins.

“I am also dying of thirst. And I think I hear a fiddle playing somewhere.” Ophelia got up from the bed. “I’m coming with you.”

He frowned. “If you want to avoid trouble, maybe it would be best to stay out of saloons. Look what happened when you cut my hair.”

“I don’t care. I’m not staying here by myself. I want to eat, drink, and be merry. Come on, let’s go find Charlie.”

Zeke frowned. “I’ve had about enough of Charlie. Maybe we could lose him for a while.”

“Zeke, without him I never would have found you.”

He nodded in resigned agreement. “Fair enough. Come on then.”

They found Charlie in the saloon next to the hotel, staring at what appeared to be a small picture in his hand. He was oblivious to the violin player imploring him for a tip, or even to Ophelia and Zeke standing right in front of him. He finally noticed them and quickly tucked the picture into his right pocket. The worn handbill, which he carried in his left pocket, sat on the table in front of him next to a glass of ale.

Ophelia nodded at the handbill with the two men staring out as if daring anyone to catch them. "Charlie, we could've been those two men standing right in front of you, and you wouldn't have noticed because you were so focused on the photo you just slipped into your pocket." Ophelia teased him to cover her insecurity. "Who's in the picture—your sweetheart?"

Charlie smirked and shook his head. "I only have eyes for you, Ophelia." He smiled at her, batted his lashes, winked, then turned his attention toward Ezekiel and gave a start. "I hardly recognized you."

"I'll take that as a compliment," said Zeke. He sat at the table and looked around. "Will someone come over, or do I need to retrieve libations from the bar?"

In the excitement of seeing Zeke in his new clothes, Ophelia hadn't paid much attention to her own appearance. The sulfurous bathwater aroma clung to her skin, and her hair was a tangled mess. For Charlie's sake, she wished she'd at least combed and pinned her hair. But it was just as well not to look pretty and draw attention. Who needed pretty in a rough mining town? Pretty could be an advantage if you played it right. But pretty could also lead to trouble. From watching Pearl die and seeing other women age, Ophelia knew that pretty didn't last. If Charlie only liked her when she was pretty, it was best to lose him now.

Pearl had spent hours tugging at Ophelia's hair and painting her face to make her look nice so that she could pluck the gold from men's pockets. Ophelia's mother had also tugged and braided her hair; she'd even tied velvet ribbons into it. What was the point of all that primping in Grafton, the middle of nowhere, where most of the men were as old as her father? Although Ophelia had no use for pretty, her current state of odiferous dishevelment embarrassed her.

Despite Ezekiel's dapper attire, no one came over to serve him, so he went to the bar and came back with two bottles of ale, which were—miraculously—cold. Ophelia took a long thirsty swallow. By the time her ale was gone, she didn't care about the way she looked and smelled anymore. She smiled at Zeke. After a decade of estrangement, they were together again. And she had enough money to keep them out of trouble.

The smell of grilled meat wafted to them from the back of the saloon. Soot-faced miners filtered in, some still carrying their helmets, pickaxes, and lunch pails. A general clamor filled the place, and the saloonkeeper stood on the bar and hollered the dinner special. Ophelia, Charlie, and Zeke ate right there in the saloon: meat, beans, and cornbread, washed down with more ale. After subsisting mostly on wild game for days, the simple saloon fare tasted delicious. The plates were collected in big metal washtubs, and the fiddler played again, this time accompanied by a banjo.

The two men played "Hard Times." And before long someone started to sing. Others joined, and a few others. At the chorus, the whole saloon sang as one:

" 'Tis the song, the sigh of the weary,
Hard Times, hard times, come again no more.
Many days you have lingered around my cabin
door;
Oh! Hard times come again no more."

Every man, even the broken, the outcasts, and the lame, became brethren in that song. It was the hour of spirited revelry and camaraderie before card games are played and lost; before someone is accused of cheating; before drunken brawls; before reason ends and killing begins. Charlie wiped a tear from the corner of his eye. Ophelia put her hand on top of his. They'd all had hard times at some point in their lives.

When whiskey replaced the ale and men's glassy-eyed gazes wandered in malice to other men and in lust to the few saloon girls and soiled doves brave—or stupid or desperate—enough to ply their trade in Frisco, Ophelia made herself smaller and squeezed between Zeke and Charlie. They left the saloon just before the dissolution and slept soundly at the Sand Friend Sicko Inn.

In the morning, they awoke cotton-mouthed and groggy, with pounding heads, listening to a distant steam whistle blowing. They made it to the station just in time to catch the train.

Six

Luther scanned the newspaper, but the words made no sense, thanks to damned Ophelia. Ever since he'd heard the news she'd been seen in Grafton, he couldn't concentrate. He slammed the paper down on his desk. Through the open door of his study, he could see his two wives setting the dining room table. The senior wife whom he mentally called *The Widow,* but verbally called "Yes, Dear," stood behind the younger wife, inspecting, scolding, and correcting her every move.

The Widow's unshakable composure had always irritated him, because it gave her an air of superiority. He chuckled with satisfaction as she threw up her hands and ordered the pregnant young dolt out of the room. The way this girl ruffled the Widow's feathers brought Luther some much needed amusement. The Widow smoothed her skirt, patted her hair into place, and entered his study. The tight smile pasted on her face accentuated the vein at her temple, which appeared on the rare occasions when she was angry.

She sighed, put her hands on her hips, and shook her head. "That girl is a nincompoop! I hope the father of that baby she's carrying has some wits, or we could all be in trouble."

"Does anyone know who the father is?" he asked.

She looked at the floor. "I'm afraid not."

"Have you asked her?"

She paused for a moment, then looked at him. "No. Perhaps it is better that we don't know. I'll pray on it instead." She walked behind his chair and began rubbing his shoulders.

His muscles melted under her touch. He groaned and closed his eyes.

"Thank you for helping my brother by taking that dim-witted daughter of his as your second wife. Without your kindness, his reputation and the family name would've been ruined."

"As long as he keeps paying for her upkeep, I don't mind." With her magic hands and delicious cooking, the Widow had spun a web from which he could never escape.

The Widow sniffed and stopped rubbing his shoulders. "Do I smell spirits?"

"No, dear, of course not."

She resumed rubbing. "Have you bedded her yet?" Her voice was soft but full of anticipation.

"Dearest wife, I never wanted to be a cock in a henhouse. In fact, I never wanted to marry at all. But you were kind to me when I was wounded and broken."

"And broke," she added.

He pulled away and glared at her. "What did you say?"

"Broke, broken, yes, it's all the same. The Lord placed me in your service for a reason—to save you. And in this life, I will always be in your service, but not eternally. I'm glad that doesn't bother you."

He stood, grimaced, and tried not to show how much this talk annoyed him. Instead of reacting with a slap, he'd later use her self-professed servitude to coax her into performing forbidden acts, the kind that would cause the gaggle of relief-society ladies who habitually gathered in their parlor to gasp. In the celestial order of Mormondom, his conversion had somehow advanced her heavenly standing, so she was as indebted to him as he was to her.

He went to the window and watched a young couple strolling by. The man picked a rose from one of their hedges and handed it to his lady. The thieving bastard. Luther lifted the window and was about to yell, hoping the commotion might distract the Widow from her line of questioning about the girl.

"So, what was it like—to lie with her?" she asked.

Forgetting about the rose thief, he turned from the window, walked over to her, crossed his arms, and gave her a scrutinizing look. "Do I detect a note of jealousy? The girl's condition is repulsive. I have no desire for her like that." He uncrossed his arms and scratched his head. "You've had sister-wives before. Surely you must be accustomed to this kind of arrangement. Did you often ask your first husband for a description of his relations with your sister-wives?"

She sniffed, stiffened her neck, and straightened in a pathetic gesture to maintain her dignity. "It wasn't like this back then. There wasn't as much difference in our ages." She patted her hair and bit her lip. "And I was always the prettiest one."

"I'll say it again. I never wanted to be a cock in a henhouse. This wasn't my idea."

He strode to his desk and removed the bottle of fine scotch he kept in the drawer."

"Luther!"

He held his hand up to her and wagged his finger. "Ah, ah, ah . . ." He shook his head. "You and this ridiculous conversation have driven me to it." He poured a shot, downed it, and felt better. "Ahh, but now that we're on the subject, I'll confess. I was looking forward to bedding her and maybe providing a little discipline for her wayward ways." He raised his eyebrows a couple of times and winked at the Widow. She frowned and blushed. Her discomfort at his drinking and open talk excited him. "Unfortunately, now that she's here, I'm afraid I find her presence as irritating as you do. Maybe once she's had the baby, I'll be able to enjoy bedding her."

At that, the Widow straightened and appeared nervous. She

moved closer to him and whispered, "She's as stubborn as a mule. I think she'll need a very stern hand. Try not to show her any tenderness. She'll see it as weakness. That's how it is with these types of girls."

He nodded in agreement, licked his lips, and suppressed a groan of pleasure. Jealousy had brought out the devil in the Widow—jealousy over him.

The Widow brushed and patted his lapel with her fingers. "Speaking of girls," she said, "What about Ophelia? It's unbelievable that, after all this time, she suddenly appears in the Grafton cemetery at her parents' grave. Do you think Mrs. Thompson is telling the truth? It must be killing you to think Ophelia could have been in Grafton after you spent all those fruitless years searching for her."

Damn—Ophelia again. He'd been relishing the Widow's jealous insecurity and had for a few moments been free of Ophelia. "Thoughts of Ophelia are driving me mad," he said.

"I can write a letter to my cousin in California. Do you have a picture? It would certainly help. Why, maybe we can make circulars."

He put his hands on her shoulders and steered her toward a chair. "I have something to tell you, and I think you should be seated."

She tried to wriggle out of his grasp. "No, Luther, I don't want to sit. Dinner's almost ready. What is it?"

He pushed her into the chair and leaned over it, using his large frame to bar her departure. He tasted the last lingering drop of scotch on his lips and panted over her like a teasing hyena about to devour its prey. She grimaced and turned her head. He cupped her chin in his hand and turned her face toward his. "Ophelia shot me." He watched with pleasure as her eyes went wide with horror and her whole body tensed.

"And then she tricked the cowhand into stealing all the

money and running off with her."

The Widow squirmed. A small bead of sweat ran down her temple. The room was hot, and he made it hotter by hovering over her. He was sweating, too. A drop of his sweat landed on her apron.

"No, Luther. Ophelia wouldn't do that. Why, those vile spirits are talking now." She glared at the bottle on his desk as if it were a demon. "That wasn't your first drink. I smelled it when I came in. You can't 'no, dear' me that easily." She tapped the tip of her nose. "The nose always knows. Now, why on earth do you think Ophelia shot you? When it happened, you said you had no idea where the bullet came from."

He stopped hovering over her, knelt down in front of her, and clamped his hands over her thighs.

She gasped and tensed. "Luther!"

"I saw them standing down by the river, soaking wet, barely clothed, their young quivering bodies rubbing against each other, lips touching, kissing so deeply and passionately, they didn't even notice me until I fired a round in the air."

She blinked several times, then tried to loosen her dress collar to free herself from the chair. He kept his grip on her thighs. More trickles of sweat rolled down her temple.

"What do you think of that? Young, sweet Ophelia shot me." His knees ached, so he stood, stretched, and went over to his desk for another shot of scotch. His head twitched and he sighed long and loud, deriving pleasure from both the scotch and the horror-stricken look frozen on the Widow's face. "That's why I let the cowhand go." He looked at her, narrowed his eyes, and nodded. "We must find Ophelia. And she must pay for her crimes."

Seven

The Doll House, however full of ghosts and bad memories, was a welcome respite from nearly a month of horse and rail travel. The bathtub, bed, clean linens, kitchen, and privy were luxuries Ophelia had taken for granted until her trip.

By redecorating, she had tried to erase the house's illicit past and turn it into an ordinary boarding house. Gone were the gaudy Romanesque nudes, the burgundy velvet chaise lounges, and all traces of the exotic or erotic. The house was now adorned with gingham and lace: pastoral scenes, milkmaids, statues of pink-cheeked, cherubic children—wholesome America. Oh, but it was like putting lipstick on a pig and seemed to her such a façade. The house would never be legitimate, and neither would she.

She showed Zeke to a bedroom on the second floor as far away from Charlie's room as possible. The stairs to her attic sanctuary creaked under her tired feet. She liked the attic's slanted ceiling, and the turret that formed a steeple overhead. In summer, it was sometimes unbearably hot, so she would crawl out her window and sleep on the roof under the stars. The attic had always been her hideaway from the world.

She dropped her coach bag, opened both windows, and felt the cross breeze stir the stuffy air. After much unlacing, wriggling, and cajoling, her dress and underclothes fell to the floor in a heap. She leaned into the full-length mirror, so she could release the clasp of the ruby necklace. Relieved and naked, she lay down on her bed next to Dolly, her old, tattered, one-eyed ragdoll, who despite her shabby state, sat primly on the bed propped by lace-trimmed pillows.

Ophelia held the necklace up to a ray of sunlight and inspected the rubies. Dolly had aged and been ravaged by time. But the stones hadn't. Maybe that's why they were so precious. Ophelia wanted to know not only the necklace's monetary value, but also the story behind it. What had happened between her mother and her uncle that he'd come to hate her so much over the necklace?

She feared it had been a mistake to visit Grafton. Mrs. Thompson had a big mouth and would spread the news. Luther was bound to hear it. Then what? Would he look for her? Charlie was smart to tell folks they were living in California. Maybe after hearing that they lived in California, Luther would decide not to look for her, at least not in Ogden. But what if she had the misfortune of running into him? After Pearl's death, she'd started using her real name instead of Miss Peach. Now she realized that had been a mistake.

She turned Dolly over, stuffed the necklace into the secret gash in her back, and rearranged her stuffing. Dolly had been through a lot of hard times, and the years had not been kind to her. After Ophelia dressed and went back downstairs, she found Nell in the kitchen, doubled over and coughing so hard, she had to lean on her broom for support. Ophelia tried to remove the broom from her hands and guide her to a seat, but the old woman shook her head, continued her coughing fit, and refused to loosen her death grip on the broom.

Zeke stood in the doorway and watched. "I tried to help her," he whispered.

Nell shook her head, waved them off, and shuffled, coughing, all the way out of the room into the back garden.

"She's going to work herself to death," Ophelia said. "I tried to hire more help, but she wouldn't hear of it—insists on doing everything herself. Her coughing probably scared the lodger away. I don't see him anywhere."

Zeke shook his head. "No, he's still here. I saw him earlier. Ran into him when I was half-dressed coming out of the bath." He grinned. "I think I scared him." He sat at the kitchen table and drummed his hand on top of it three times. "Ophelia, I'm not a freeloader. This place needs some repairs. Put me to work. I'll even do women's work, so I don't have to watch that poor old lady hobble around coughing to death. Is she blind too?"

Ophelia sat at the table with him. "Only partially. I'd love your help with some of the repairs. The truth is, we may need to sell this house and move somewhere else. What do you think about that?" She got up. "Make yourself at home here. I store most perishables in the basement because there's a big root-cellar down there completely closed off with a heavy door. I'll show it to you in a minute. Would you like a cup of tea or something to eat?"

"Yes, thank you. I'll have a cup of tea." Zeke looked around the room. "Ophelia, this is the nicest house I've ever been a guest at. You've done well. Why do you want to sell it?" He narrowed his eyes and gave her an unnerving look. "Are you worried about Luther? If he comes anywhere near you or this house, I'll kill him."

Ophelia sighed, put the teapot on the stove, sat back down, cupped her chin in her hand, and studied the table. Before answering, she looked at him. "First of all, you're not a guest. This is your home. Second, I'm not afraid of Luther coming around here because Charlie had the presence of mind to tell Mrs. Thompson that we live in California. So he won't be looking for me here. What I'm worried about is you seeking revenge. If we move out of the territory, perhaps that won't be a temptation."

The back door opened and they heard Nell coughing. Ophelia made a horrified face and stared at Zeke until the coughing subsided. "Good Lord, I don't know what would happen to Nell if we sold the house and moved. I'm not sure she's healthy enough to move anywhere, except down the road. Maybe she'd make it to Corinne."

Eight

Ophelia sat at Pearl's desk in the study and stared at the ledger. In the five months she'd been operating a boarding house, she hadn't grossed as much as the Doll House had averaged in one night. Not having a steady stream of income made her nervous. A picture of Pearl sat on the desk and reminded Ophelia that her fear of not having enough savings had been partially inherited from her.

She still didn't know exactly how much Pearl had left her. Stacks of ledgers were piled on the desk and she needed to study them before she met with the lawyer again. He'd been Pearl's lawyer and was hers now, but she didn't entirely trust him. She didn't entirely trust anyone, except for Zeke and maybe Charlie. The ledgers and financial documents overwhelmed her. She stared at them in dismay, wondering where to start. Someone knocked softly on the study door.

"Come in," said Ophelia.

It was the lodger, hat in hand, and suitcase on the floor. She rose and beckoned him to the chair in front of her desk. "Good morning."

The study, decorated by Pearl, was one of the few rooms Ophelia hadn't changed because it was completely masculine and displayed no hints of anything erotic. When Pearl was occupied in the study, she'd dropped her feminine charm. Stuffed pheasants and ducks, trophies from one of her hunting outings with Emily Browning, were mounted on the wall. It'd been her masculine place, and in it she'd been all business. Ophelia often stared at the picture of Pearl on the desk and tried to conjure her guidance in matters of business, for which she'd had an uncanny knack.

Ophelia looked at the lodger's bag. "Are you leaving us?"

He sat and looked around the room rather than at Ophelia. "I've been called back to Chicago."

She glanced at the ledger and back up to him. "Oh, I see. You've already paid through the end of the month. I can refund—"

"Keep it. The company is paying."

"Well, thank you. Was everything satisfactory? Did we meet your expectations?"

He coughed and cleared his throat. "Everything was satisfactory. I was expecting a little more . . . uh, well . . . how should I put this? My wife died last September, and I've been feeling a little lonely." He looked at her, checking for understanding.

"I see. So you were maybe expecting female company because perhaps you'd heard somewhere that sort of thing was available here?"

He nodded and looked down.

She peered at the ledger, sighed, and saw his name printed. "Mr. Williams, do you realize that the amount you paid for an entire month's lodging would barely be enough for one night with a lady at the former establishment?"

He met her gaze, wide-eyed, mouth slightly agape. "No. I didn't know it was that expensive. That's quite a business. And men paid that much?"

She regarded him gently with pity and nodded. "Yes, surprising though it may be, there are a lot of lonely rich men out there, many of whom are married. The Doll House was very exclusive, and what we thought was a discreet establishment, mostly invitation only. I'm surprised you know about it. Where did you—oh, never mind." She looked at him with concern. "Anyway, I'm sorry about your wife."

He nodded sadly and looked at the floor again. If she didn't know better, she'd say he wasn't the type. But she knew better. They were all the type. He was probably lying about his wife. But she pitied him all the same. She tapped her fingers on the desk, sighed, opened a drawer, and pulled out a calling card. Before she handed it to him, she gazed at it, and looked back at him.

He stared at her and the card with anticipation.

"When we closed, it was quite a loss for the girls who worked here. There's nothing else quite like the old Doll House in Ogden anymore. But this is just a boarding house now, so please make sure to explain that to anyone you might know who believes otherwise. Now I don't usually do this, but I'm going to give you this card. Rose is one of the best—expensive, but worth every penny, so don't try to negotiate." She held out the card. When he reached for it, she grabbed his wrist with her other hand and stared at him intensely. "If anything happens to her as a result of your visit, I'll hunt you down and kill you." She let go of his wrist and smiled.

Charlie entered the room with a cup of coffee and a newspaper tucked under his arm. From the look on his face, Ophelia thought he must have heard her comment to the lodger. The lodger stood. His face registered shock. He hadn't taken hold of the card yet.

"You understand I have to tell you that as a precautionary warning because there are some bad men out there, Mr. Williams." She wiggled the card, indicating he should take it and be gone.

He took it from her cautiously and held it in awe. "Thank you," he whispered. He slipped the card into his pocket, tipped his hat to her, picked up his suitcase, and left.

Charlie stared at the door through which the man had made his hasty exit. "Ophelia," he said.

She looked at him. "Shhh!"

He smirked and shook his head. "I'll hunt you down and kill you." He chuckled.

"Quiet."

He spread the newspaper on a small writing desk, peered at it, and took a sip of his coffee. "Are you becoming a john, Ophelia?" he asked without looking at her, as if he were commenting on the weather.

"No, of course not. But that man came here expecting to meet some ladies. His wife is dead, and he's lonely. Plus, most of the girls who worked here don't have a suitable place to go for employment, and I feel bad about that."

"Bad enough to reopen?"

"Don't be silly. Why don't you stop teasing me and get to work on your book, sir."

Almost a month had passed since they'd returned to Ogden. Up until that point, all three of them had lived lives full of danger and drama. Adjusting to the safety and tranquility of domestic life was more difficult than Ophelia, Zeke, or Charlie had imagined it would be. After recovering from their adventure, restlessness filled them, and they moved through the days with the tense, controlled movements of caged animals.

Even the house seemed bored. Once filled with flirtatious exchanges and the constant creak and groan of bedsprings, the house now seemed to tremble with quiet tension and unfulfilled desire. Wallpaper peeled and paint chipped from ennui. The pieces dropped onto the floor and startled the cat. Nell's coughing reverberated like muted thunder and shook the walls. Outside the decaying house, flowers bloomed with life and fragrance teased them outdoors.

They occupied themselves and tried to settle into domestic routines. Charlie worked on his book. Ophelia spent hours attempting to make sense of her finances, until frustration drove her to secretly start writing down stories from her own life. Ezekiel repaired the front gate and the squeaky door, and was about to undertake scraping the wallpaper, when he lost all enthusiasm. He'd taken to sleeping in the carriage house. From the study window, Ophelia would watch him emerge each morning, relieve himself on the hedges, and then go back inside. What had driven him from the house? Nell's coughing? Charlie? Or maybe—and the possibility terrified her—he was using opium again. Losing him that way, and seeing the spirit leave the body before it physically died, would be the hardest of all possible deaths for her to witness.

In the evenings, Charlie lingered by the stairs leading up to her attic bedroom where she would plant a cordial peck on his cheek and say goodnight. She never invited him up to her bedroom. And she hadn't kissed him on the lips since the hotel in Silver Reef. With so little affection from her, how long would he continue his stay? She'd been a whore for too long and didn't believe he could truly love her.

In the mornings, Charlie carried a steaming coffee cup into the study and settled down at what had become his desk. He figured he could make a fortune writing books about his life as a cowboy detective and his exploits driving cattle on the Chisholm Trail. Barbed wire had divided the open range, and with the transcontinental railroad in place for over a decade, the Western Frontier was almost history.

Although Charlie was a great storyteller, he could barely read the smudged words scribbled in the worn diary he'd carried with him for so many years, and he struggled to put his stories on paper. Ophelia had found a pair of abandoned spectacles and given them to him. He took them reluctantly, but once he realized they made it easier for him to decipher his journal, he began to wear them while he worked. She often stole a glance at his eyes, magnified behind the glasses. Inspired by his progress, she continued writing down her memories.

Ophelia stared at the door through which Mr. Williams, her last and only lodger, had exited. She looked down at the ledger and shook her head. "Running a boarding house isn't very profitable. I don't know how women survive with this as their only income."

"Many respectable boarding houses turn into cathouses for just that reason," said Charlie. He pushed his feet against the desk, tipped back his chair, and glanced out the window. "Do you really believe that man lost his wife, Ophelia?"

"Does it matter?" She noticed the way he was sitting and shook her head. "If you were a child and I was a teacher, I'd give you the cane for sitting like that!" She returned her attention to the ledgers.

Charlie became alert and stared at her intently. "Oh, please do. I think I might enjoy that."

She glanced at him, smirked, shook her head again, and tried to concentrate on the numbers in front of her.

Charlie fished in his pocket and removed a tin of cigarettes. Ophelia looked at the tin and raised her eyebrows. He set it down on the desk without opening it. A breeze carried scents of lilac and a meadowlark's song through the window. Dappled sunlight in the billowing curtains behind him created such a contrasting backdrop to his salt-of-the-earth solidity, it made her smile.

He met her smile with a grin. "Ophelia, would you come over and read this for me? I could use your advice."

She glanced at him, then at the papers on her desk, pretending to study them. "Only if you remove your feet from the desk and sit properly."

He sat straight in his chair and folded his hands in front of him, imitating a well-behaved schoolboy. Grateful for a distraction, she stood, walked over, and looked at his paper. He rose from his chair, moved close behind her, tucked a loose strand of her hair behind her ear, and whispered so close that she felt his breath on her skin. "What do you think?"

She froze and stared at the blank page.

He wrapped his arms around her waist, pulled her toward him, and ever so softly kissed her neck. She stood still and continued staring at the blank page. He continued to kiss her neck. She closed her eyes.

The opposing desires to dissolve into his kisses and run out of the room immobilized her. Without urgency, his gentle caresses moved from the nape of her neck to her collarbone. His hands roamed aimlessly over her tight corset, which she would soon stop wearing forever. Her ribs wanted to be free. She wanted to be free. She turned and kissed him. Her head dropped back and her spine arched. A cautious ache swelled between her legs.

Why not? Why not give in to this passion? She was not a vestal virgin, nor a chaste wife, nor a virtuous woman. She was unmarried and beholden to no one. Her reputation was already ruined. Why not enjoy herself in Charlie's arms? They were, after all, friends. He was her ally. From the day she'd first seen him, she'd been attracted to the mischievous look in his eyes. The day was hot, and he'd rolled up his shirtsleeves. She traced a bulging vein on his sinewy forearm with her finger, then buried her face in his chest.

He took her chin in his strong hand and gently lifted her face toward his. He kissed her again, at first softly, then deeper. She'd never been kissed or caressed in such a way. Time froze. Each point of contact between them was a tiny tinge of ecstasy, electric, magnetic, and, for the moment—all that mattered.

There was no throbbing urgency, no clock ticking toward penetration, toward ejaculation, toward his pleasure.

And, for the first time, it was as if she actually mattered. Charlie didn't see her as an object to be viewed, played with, prodded, and penetrated, but as a real person with feelings and sensations of her own. It was as if all parts of her mattered—from her eyelids, which he brushed softly with his lips, to her fingers, which he kissed and rubbed across his cheek. When she looked into his eyes, it was as if he saw her, saw her soul, as it was, as it should be, with love and no torment.

He was different from any man she'd ever known, and yet familiar. She remembered him cradling her in his arms when she was sick in the desert. She saw him riding next to her mile after mile, through sage country and piñon mesas, passing below snow-capped mountain peaks. Ophelia remembered his eyes while he played the harmonica, and she sang under the stars on their way to Silver Reef. He had been there all along, but she had failed to fully see him. Charlie, Detective Sirringo, full of humor, and stories, and vitality, and light; he had led her to Ezekiel.

And yet she pulled away from his deep kiss. She didn't deserve his loving caresses, the pleasure or happiness they brought. She briefly pressed her head into his chest again and then turned toward the half-opened door. "Charlie, someone might see," she whispered.

"Who?" he asked

"Nell, Zeke, a prospective lodger."

"Does it matter?"

"Yes." She stared at the door as if Frankenstein's monster might come through it.

Charlie regarded her expression and then looked at the door. "Why don't I close it then?"

He let her go, crossed the room, and closed the door. The

brief separation made her uncertain. He rushed back and began to fumble with the buttons on her dress. She had once dressed for ultimate accessibility. The respectable dress she now wore was designed to deter passion. It was hot and uncomfortable, and she wanted to rip it off, but didn't want to appear too eager. When she was finally naked, she felt chilled, even though the air was warm. She helped Charlie free himself from his shirt. His skin under the shirt was much whiter than his sun-browned hands and face. She pressed her cheek against a small pelt of dark chest hair. He held her and stroked her head.

And then he kissed her with all the pent-up energy of a cowboy who'd been spending too much time indoors. He hoisted her onto the desk. When their bodies joined she surrendered and didn't transport her mind to some other place as she so often had with men. She felt the rhythm of him inside her until they both cried out. And then the inevitable awkward separation occurred. What a beautiful, filthy, sacred, and profane act, at once natural and unnatural, that would forever change the quality of their togetherness.

It wasn't until later, as she washed in the tub, that she felt dirty and ashamed and realized in her ecstasy, she had completely forgotten the French preventives. She sank down until her head was submerged and ran her hands over her skull. Could the shape of her cranium really foretell her destiny and nature? Only one type of woman was said to enjoy sexual activities. Maybe the doctor had been right about her.

NINE

After the affair with Charlie began, Ophelia traded tight-laced corsets and fashionable bustles for flowing and comfortable Bohemian-style dresses. It was a style popular in Paris and advocated by the Rational Dress Society. She had tried to be a proper lady, and it hadn't suited her one bit. Whether or not Charlie loved her was entirely up to him. She wouldn't pretend anymore that she was proper, or fashionable, or a lady. She didn't need anyone's approval. She was wealthy and had been reunited with her brother. They were kin, and kin came before lovers.

Yet she could no longer ignore her sexual feelings. If society deemed her a whore, so be it. Women around the nation were increasingly calling for their right to vote. When would they call for their right to love whom they wanted and wear trousers without public ridicule?

She wanted to go to the local National Women's Suffrage Association meetings, but although admirable, many of the women were tight-laced prudes. Once one of them discovered her past, word spread like wildfire. Most of them, whether Mormon or not, came from wealthy, upper-class backgrounds. They didn't seem to understand how some women had to do all manner of things to survive. The charity ladies gladly took her donations, but she was met with icy stares whenever she attended public events. She pretended to have a thick sin, but underneath, she couldn't bare the shame and often dreamed of moving somewhere else and starting a new life.

She focused on the house and her work in the study with Charlie. They often took a break from their work and did a little horizontal folk dancing. Charlie didn't like the French preventives, but he was familiar with them and agreed to use them anyway. She figured that most of his experience with women came from visiting brothels. How else? He had never mentioned a wife.

One hot afternoon, they decided to walk to the new ice cream parlor on Fifth Street. Ophelia wore a loose-fitting dress and tucked her hair under a bonnet. After Ogden became the hub of rail travel, it had gradually transformed from a small shanty town to a bustling city with a few fancy hotels and a mule-drawn railcar. Some of the mansions on the hill even had plumbing and telephones. Word around town was that within a year, electricity would replace the gas lamps. They stopped to admire the new Broom Hotel. Fifth Street was no longer an open den of illicit activity. Shops, hotels, and restaurants catered to respectable travelers and businessmen. Illicit activities still took place, but not as openly, and many seemingly legitimate establishments had underground gambling and prostitution operations.

London's Ice Cream Parlor was so new that the picture-glass window still sparkled. Three girls and two boys sat outside on wooden benches intently licking their cones. The younger boy, still in knee breeches, lacked licking skills and his scoop tumbled to the ground after he pushed it too hard with his tongue. He wailed in frustration and tried to pick it up. The chocolate ice cream had merged with dirt and looked like the bowels of a goose had let loose down his arm.

His mother gasped in horror, yanked him by his clean arm, and commanded him to release what was left of the sticky mess. The boy howled at the top of his lungs while his mother cautiously tried to smack him without sullying her hand. An immaculately dressed young lady wearing a lace apron and a lovely ivory brooch emerged from the ice-cream parlor with a wet rag in her hand. She calmly approached the boy and his mother with the clean white rag.

"May I?" she asked the mother.

The mother let go of the boy's arm and stepped back, disapproval set firmly in her jaw. The young lady knelt and spoke softly to the small boy. "Now if you stop crying, and let me clean you, I'll get you another ice-cream cone."

The boy gulped the air, stopped crying, and stared at the lady as if she were an angel. She cleaned off his goopy arm, took him by the hand, and led him back into the ice-cream parlor. The mother smiled tightly, nodded thanks to the lady, and tended to the rest of her brood.

Charlie and Ophelia exchanged amused glances. Ophelia nodded to the unappetizing chocolate mess melting in the dirt. "I think I'll get strawberry," she mumbled to Charlie.

The lady behind the counter handed the little boy a new cone and turned her attention toward them. She stared at Ophelia and squinted, as if trying to recognize her. Ophelia stared at the beautiful brooch attached to the throat of her high-necked blouse and wondered why she was so formally dressed and not soaked with perspiration from running around on such a hot day. She and Charlie both ordered strawberry cones.

The lady looked at Ophelia and smiled. "When the peach crop comes in, I'll have peach ice cream. Have you ever tried peach ice cream?" she asked.

She put such emphasis on the word *peach,* Charlie and Ophelia glanced at each other, both wondering if she knew something. They smiled at her politely and shook their heads. "No, can't say I have," said Charlie.

"It's delicious. You'll have to come back when peaches are in season." She smiled and handed them their cones.

They sat at a table in the corner and licked the strawberry ice cream. Ophelia licked around the side of the cone and at the same time tried to cement it in place with her tongue, so it wouldn't topple off like the little boy's. Charlie stared at her and licked without much strategy. His large tongue was as pink as a dog's. Ophelia imagined Charlie's scoop toppling. Would the ice-cream lady replace his too?

Soon the customers were gone and the lady swept the floor. She kept glancing at Ophelia and smiling. A large man thumped down from upstairs and stood at the ice-cream parlor entrance. He straightened his tie, gave the young lady a satisfied smile, and pressed something into her hand.

Charlie was facing Ophelia and hadn't noticed the exchange. Ophelia stopped mid-lick and stared at the lady. She winked at Ophelia and resumed sweeping.

Ophelia could usually spot such an operation a mile away, but this had caught her off-guard, and she was impressed. This lady was simultaneously working both sides of society with seamless ease. The street was still the street. She and Charlie finished their cones, wiped their mouths with napkins, and walked toward the door.

The ice-cream lady called to Ophelia. "Excuse me, Miss. May I have a quick word?"

Ophelia glanced at Charlie.

"I'm going to have a smoke outside. Take your time," he said.

Ophelia glanced up the stairs and looked at the lady.

The lady put her hand to the side of her mouth and whispered, "We've got ice cream downstairs and tarts upstairs."

"Why are you telling me this?" asked Ophelia.

"Because you're the famous Miss Peach, and I've wanted to meet you ever since I moved here. I'm thrilled to finally make your acquaintance." She held her hand out. "Belle London."

Ophelia didn't take her hand. "I'm not Miss Peach anymore. I'm Ophelia Oatman. And I run a respectable lodging house, which I'm thinking of selling so I can move to a town where I can go out for ice cream without anyone recognizing me. I'd very much like the past to remain in the past. How did you even know who I was? Oh, never mind." Ophelia sighed.

The woman's eyes grew wide with excitement. "You mean the Doll House? It might be for sale? Oh, we must talk. I'm very interested."

They moved out of the doorway, so a man and a lady could enter. Belle smiled at them. "Welcome to London's Ice Cream Parlor. I'll be right with you." Her expression was excitement tinged with mischief. "Oh, we must talk. I'll come to the house Thursday, midmorning. Will you be available?"

Ophelia hesitated. She didn't want to associate with a madam and be reminded of her former life. And yet just the other day, she'd been acting the madam herself by giving out a girl's calling card. The truth was that Belle London might be the only person in town who'd actually purchase her house, considering its history. "Very well, that's fine," said Ophelia managing a weak, resigned smile.

Ophelia could still smell the vapors of Charlie's cigarette lingering in the stagnant air.

"What was that all about? She seems like a nice young lady. Certainly sells delicious ice cream," said Charlie.

Ophelia moved close to Charlie and whispered in his ear. "She's a madam. Ice cream downstairs, tarts upstairs!"

Charlie looked shocked. "How do you know?"

"Female intuition, and she told me."

He looked dumbfounded and disappointed. "I didn't notice a single thing off-kilter."

"Maybe you've lost your touch, Detective Sirringo. Maybe

it's time to retire and focus on your book."

Charlie looked at Ophelia. "I've resigned; I'm not retired. To retire is to expire, and I won't do that."

"Well, it's quite a shocking operation with children so close. I guess you can get away with just about anything as long as you dress well."

"Now, come on, you can't judge her for expanding her scope. There's not much profit in ice cream, especially with every little Tommy Towhead dropping his scoop in the dirt."

The way Charlie emphasized the word *you* really stung. She'd never escape her past. Even Charlie wouldn't let her forget it. "No, of course I can't judge her. But all the same, we kept our establishment quite separate from children. Imagine if we'd had a schoolhouse out back."

Charlie's cavalier eyes danced with merriment and mischief, "The boys would probably stay in school a lot longer."

Ophelia laughed. Charlie wasn't a righteous man. Even though he'd arrested plenty of outlaws and brought them before judges, he was no judge. He'd said many times that landing on the right side of the law had been a lucky break; he could've just as easily wound up a criminal because he'd been a hot-headed youth and almost killed someone in a fight on more than one occasion.

"She'll be calling at the house on Thursday morning."

He raised his brows, then furrowed them. "For what business?" he asked.

"Don't worry, Charlie. I'm not reviving my old ways. She has a peculiar fascination with the house, and I'm starting to think I might sell it."

"Sell the Doll House? Where would you live?"

"The lodging house. Please don't call it the Doll House or refer to it as a parlor house anymore. That's part of the reason I want to sell it. As long as I live there, I'll never escape the past.

I don't know. I might buy something else, farther from town, or maybe somewhere entirely different. Maybe it's time to get out of the Utah Territory and live in the United States."

"A ranch in Texas or New Mexico Territory would sure be nice. I know that country." He smiled and chewed the side of his mustache as if there were still some ice cream on it.

"Charlie, you're eating your mustache again. Maybe you should shave it off."

Ten

Ophelia watched from the window as Belle London approached the house. Belle assessed the rickety gate, the garden, and the front porch. Ezekiel had set about to fixing the place and had made a few improvements before a melancholy spirit overtook him and his enthusiasm for labor disappeared. He spent most of his time in the carriage house wearing his old clothes, hardly talking to anyone. Ophelia worried that he was drinking all day or, worse, had picked up the opium habit again.

Although Fifth Street was a bit more refined than it had been in the seventies, there were still plenty of places where a person could buy opium. Perhaps she had uprooted him from his former existence too fast. At least while working for Mr. Gee, Zeke had been occupied and was not using opium. The elation of their reunion and the novelty of Ogden had worn off, and he now seemed to be drifting into old habits.

Ophelia straightened her hair in the hall mirror before she opened the door for Belle. Charlie was on one of his mysterious outings, and Zeke didn't enjoy social calls, so Ophelia asked Nell to bring tea for two. She'd given up her attempts to convince Nell to stop working and rest. The woman was unable to be idle.

When Belle London walked through the door and saw the inside of the house, her face practically dropped to the floor with disappointment. She looked as if she'd just entered a mausoleum. "I hope I'm not inconveniencing you," she said to

Ophelia. "I've been very eager to see this place and talk to you." She craned her neck, trying to see past the foyer into other rooms.

"No, of course not. Please come in. I'll give you a tour after we have tea," said Ophelia.

She led Belle into the parlor where Nell was setting out a tea tray. The plain décor of the parlor was evidently too much, and Belle deflated like a balloon.

Ophelia explained. "It's not what it once was. I took everything down and changed all the furnishings, so no one would get the wrong idea and think it was still a parlor house. It's just a lodging house now. In fact, it's hardly even that. My last border left. It's just me, my brother, Mr. Sirringo, and Nell here."

Belle continued to assess the house, but with less urgency and excitement. "What did you do with everything? The Doll House was legendary for its exotic ambiance." She looked at a wholesome landscape painting and wrinkled her nose. "Do you have anything left? Maybe I could purchase some of it. Oh, I've heard such stories. You and Pearl were famous."

"Pearl understood how to turn sex and everything associated with it into a profitable business. The success had nothing to do with me, but I did the best I could and made the most of the life. Selling female favors is a risky business. Did you hear how Pearl died? I was there holding her hand to the very end. When you witness something like that, you have to change your life."

Belle looked Ophelia straight in the eyes and lowered her voice. "I'm sorry to hear it. I'm not new to the profession, and I've seen my share of the dangers. But death comes to us all eventually. Now, do give yourself some credit for the house's success. Pearl was the head, and you were the heart. From what I've heard, you were the one who took care of the girls. She needed you, as did they."

Ophelia stared in disbelief. "Where did you hear that? I had no idea anyone knew of us outside of Ogden. Where did you say you're from, anyway? How on earth do you know about us?"

Belle smiled. "Word travels faster than the railroad. Beware the gossip train! You mustn't worry though. I was impressed with what I heard. Now that Pearl has passed and you're out of the business, maybe I can revive this grand old house. You see, I may be young, but I've already gained expertise in the business."

"So which are you? The head or the heart?" asked Ophelia.

Belle folded her hands in her lap. Her eyes twinkled and she grinned. "I'm both."

Ophelia got up to pour the tea and stopped. The air in the parlor was stale and stifling. She opened the window, felt a cool breeze, and turned toward Belle. "Let's have tea in the garden. The breeze, the blossoms, the darling little hummingbirds—they'll do us good."

Ophelia carried the tea tray. Belle held the door open for her. They settled into the back garden in white wicker chairs under a trellis of honeysuckle and wisteria vines. In a corner of the yard sat an ugly fire ring surrounded by empty whiskey bottles and broken chairs. Belle stared at the eyesore where Charlie and Ezekiel drank, smoked, and spat tobacco.

"Men!" exclaimed Ophelia, embarrassed.

Belle smiled and nodded. "Yes, they can be pigs, can't they? How did you handle them at the Doll House?"

"I'd rather not relive the past. It's hard for me to reconcile. I was raised a Saint, if you can believe that. I find it so peculiar that you know so much about us. Where did you hear about us?"

Belle ignored Ophelia's question, sipped her tea, and looked around the garden. "A little overgrown, but nice. I don't suppose it saw much use when you ran the Doll House. Hmm, perhaps there's a certain type of man who would pay extra for a romp in the garden. My plan for dealing with pigs is to have some cribs close by, somewhere to send the men who are, you know, unfit for the house. I don't want to turn them away because it's bad for business. And I'm not just talking about the loss of income. When turned away they often become violent and cause trouble. I'm sure you've experienced that."

Ophelia nodded. "Pearl owned cribs with a man named Johnny Dobbs. But he became the trouble. And she had to get rid of him. So how did you hear about us? And where are you from? How long have you been running the place above the ice-cream parlor? I'm amazed you're getting away with that."

Belle smiled demurely. "It's not propriety that counts, but the appearance of propriety. That's why I dress so prim and proper."

Coughing interrupted their conversation. Nell shuffled, out frowning at the tea tray and empty cups.

Ophelia tried to wave her away. "Nell, please, I'll get that."

Undeterred and focused, Nell picked up the tray. An explosive cough and sputter shook her body so forcefully, she had to put the tray back down for almost a minute until her coughing fit subsided. Belle looked concerned and, possibly, sickened. They watched quietly as Nell returned to the house with the tray.

Ophelia sighed, closed her eyes, and tried to summon some patience. Belle might be her only prospective buyer, so she needed to remain civil. And yet she was tired of Belle's evasiveness. "Believe it or not, Nell was a queen once, said to be very beautiful, more beautiful than Pearl. Now, please, if we're going to continue this conversation, you must tell me something about yourself, why you came to Ogden, and how you heard about us."

"Whoring is a sordid business. But it's one of the only profitable businesses women are allowed to operate. If men could figure out a way to ban women from owning brothels, they probably would. I assumed, because of polygamy, prostitution would be less popular in the Utah Territory. But it's quite the opposite."

The air was growing warm. Ophelia loosened her collar and pushed her hair back, wishing she'd pinned it up. "Many Mormons believe polygamy is divinely decreed. Non-Mormons—or, as they're called here, Gentiles—believe polygamy is a perverse justification for harems. But unlike in a harem, Mormon women are only taught domestic skills and not the art of pleasure. We had a surprising number of polygamist customers, if you can believe that." Ophelia put her hands in her lap in a gesture of impatience and raised her voice a little. "Belle, you must tell me: where are you from? And how do you know so much about the Doll House?"

Belle appeared surprised, as if this were the first time Ophelia had asked. "Oh yes, of course. When we opened our first house in Denver, I heard a man telling stories. I'd hear other men and working girls make references from time to time, so I was really curious, and I started asking questions."

"Who is *we*?"

"My husband and I. He wasn't my husband then."

"Oh, I didn't know you were married."

"Yes. It's an unfortunate fact I'd rather not dwell on." She sighed, smoothed her dress, and smiled tightly. "My husband is looking after business elsewhere, so I'm in charge of our affairs here."

"I see," said Ophelia. "Is that difficult?"

"I prefer it, actually. My husband and I often don't see eye to eye. He's a necessary evil. But because he's gone so much, it means I really must hire a trustworthy man for security."

"I've never been married," said Ophelia.

Belle gestured to the house and the yard. "If you own all this, I wouldn't even consider marriage. You could lose all your money and property through marriage."

Noise from the carriage house diverted their attention. The door swung open and Ezekiel emerged. He wore a suit and a hat and looked well-groomed, which surprised Ophelia. She narrowed her eyes and wondered where he was going. He had only worn the new clothes a couple of times since they'd arrived in Ogden. He carefully closed the carriage house door and adjusted his hat. Ophelia called to him. He looked up with what seemed feigned surprise and walked over to them.

"Mrs. London, this is my brother, Ezekiel Oatman. Ezekiel, this is Mrs. London. She's a local—merchant. In fact, she owns the new ice-cream parlor."

Recognition and something else flashed between them. Ophelia looked from Ezekiel to Belle and back. As an astute observer of human interactions, especially between men and women, she immediately sensed something between them. Had they already been acquainted?

Belle smiled a little too broadly. "Let's speak plainly. I'm a madam, and I've come to look at this old parlor house with the intention of perhaps purchasing it one day and restoring it to its former glory." She looked from Ophelia to Zeke and back again. "Excuse me. Did you say this is your brother? Mr. Oatman, you look familiar to me. Have we met somewhere before?"

Ophelia felt something happening that she couldn't control, looked at Belle suspiciously, and answered before Zeke had a chance. "Ezekiel is my half-brother. We grew up together, but ten years ago, when we were still quite young, unfortunate circumstances tore us apart. I employed Mr. Sirringo, the man I was with at the ice-cream parlor, to locate him. We are each other's only living relative. Without Mr. Sirringo's help, we probably would never have been reunited."

Zeke ever so slightly rolled his eyes. There was still animosity between him and Charlie.

"Fascinating," said Belle. She studied Ophelia and Ezekiel. "I do see a resemblance, you know."

"Really? Most people don't. You have to look very closely," said Ophelia.

"The man you were with at the ice-cream parlor is a detective? I certainly hope he's not a Pinkerton. We've had some unfortunate dealings with Pinkertons."

Zeke crossed his arms and nodded his head in agreement.

Ophelia defended Charlie. "Well, he was. Now he's retired and has no alliance or allegiance to them. All his time is focused on writing a book."

"How thrilling!" Belle turned her attention toward Zeke. "Mr. Oatman, what do you do here? It seems very quiet. Are you employed?"

"No. I'm fixing to repair a few things, but not too much actually."

"Well, with your imposing presence, you'd be just right for a security job at my establishment. Would you be interested and available for evening employment?" Belle looked from Zeke to Ophelia. "Oh, that's all right with you, isn't it?"

Zeke interrupted. "She's my sister, not my mother. I'm a grown man; I make my own decisions." He glanced at Ophelia and looked at Belle. "Yes, I'm interested. I've done similar work in Silver Reef at a gambling hall."

"Perfect. Come by this evening around seven, and I'll put you to work. The pay is very good and, of course, there are fringe benefits." She fished in her small purse, stood up, pressed a calling card into the palm of his hand, and smiled.

Ophelia tried not to show her anger or anxiety. Ezekiel needed to stop moping around the carriage house and find an occupation, but why did it have to be security at a brothel? She supposed his past and mixed race limited his work opportunities to hard labor or the underworld.

Zeke tipped his hat to Belle. "I'll see you this evening. Ophelia, I'm going to the mercantile on Fifth Street. Do you need anything?"

"Yes, actually, I do. There's a list on the kitchen table. Thank you."

They watched Ezekiel walk away. Belle clucked her tongue. "He's got a restless spirit. It's the Indian side of him. They're meant to keep moving, hunting, and following the seasons. He's a handsome one. But Lordy, what happened to his face?"

Ophelia didn't like the way Belle talked about her brother, as if he was some exotic species. "Ezekiel has never been part of a tribe. We have the same mother and were raised together. Yes, he has Indian blood, but he doesn't know the first thing about Indians. I've been trying to keep him out of trouble. Now how on earth am I going to do that with him working at your place?"

Belle shook her head "There's hardly ever trouble at any of my establishments. I pay the law enough to keep their distance. Anyway, a man like that doesn't need your protection. He needs to be free, not cooped up in a carriage house."

"Are you implying that I'm keeping him in the carriage house?"

"Oh, no. I meant no offense. Just fight the instinct to coddle him. Sometimes we don't see people clearly when we keep them too close."

Ophelia stared at Belle and tried to control her anger. "You'll be the first to know if I decide to sell the house." She rose.

Belle took the hint and followed her through the house to the front door.

Ezekiel was at the front gate. He noticed Belle and held the gate open for her.

She called to him. "Are you walking over to the street now? Let's stroll together. I'll tell you about the job!" She turned toward Ophelia and smiled. "Thank you so much for your hospitality. If you decide to sell, I'm interested. It'll take a little work to restore it to its former glory, but it can be done." She lifted her skirt and walked carefully down the porch steps, then did a quick hustle to reach Ezekiel. He followed her through the gate, closed it, and waved to Ophelia.

Ophelia watched them walk toward town together and felt her throat tighten. Inside, the house was silent except for Nell's coughing.

Eleven

Ophelia continually tried to persuade Nell to rest and relax. But Nell would shake her head, brush Ophelia away, and keep shuffling around the house doing chores and coughing, until one day she collapsed.

Charlie and Ezekiel moved a bed onto the porch attached to the study so that Ophelia could keep an eye on her during the day. Ophelia hoped rest and fresh air would help Nell's cough. With Nell so close to the study, Ophelia and Charlie's diversions were put on hold. Charlie expressed disappointment. Ophelia pointed to his desk and told him it was time to buckle down and finish his book. Besides their lack of productivity, Charlie had tired of the awkward French preventives, and she didn't want to become pregnant.

Nursing Nell brought back memories of nursing her mother, her father, and Pearl. The day before her mother had died, she'd held out her withered hand and given Ophelia the ruby necklace. The rubies had contrasted so much with her pale, paperlike skin. To Ophelia's amazement, almost ten years later, after Ophelia had thought the necklace had long ago been sold to fund the Doll House, in a similar fashion Pearl had reached out and handed her the necklace as she lay dying.

How had her mother come by such a necklace? She couldn't believe her mother would steal it. Her mother wasn't a thief. Luther was a liar. He'd journeyed all the way across the frontier from Missouri, not to help them, but in search of the necklace.

It had to be worth a fortune. If her mother had really stolen it, as Luther claimed, why would she write to him for help? Ophelia often wished her mother had never written that letter and wondered how their lives would have turned out if Luther had never arrived.

She still hadn't asked Charlie anything about his personal finances. After each of their dalliances, he had offered to marry her, and she had brushed off his proposals as jokes. Perhaps they were genuine, but she guessed they were in response to a sense of guilt or displaced propriety. Talking about money was even more difficult now that they were lovers. He wasn't paying room and board, and she still hadn't paid him for finding Ezekiel. She'd tried to discuss paying him his fee several times, but he didn't want to talk about money, and she had no idea how much she owed him. She'd also tried to give him the necklace several times, but he always refused. If he didn't want the necklace as payment, she decided she'd keep it. Anyway, the legend in her family was that whoever sold the necklace would be cursed. Why risk bad luck when she didn't need the money? The necklace was all she had left of her mother. And it was tucked safely inside Dolly, where it belonged.

After Nell fell ill, Zeke began to cook. His demeanor and disposition had changed since he'd started working for Belle London. He purchased a new tailored suit and paid a lot of attention to his appearance, cultivating a look that was at once dapper and imposing. One night he was on his way to Belle's, and Ophelia watched with concern as he secured a dagger to a sheath around his ankle.

He looked up at her. "Don't worry about me, Ophelia," he said. "Belle's place is tame compared to where I've been."

He usually returned from work early in the morning and slept until around noon, when he'd get up, drink coffee, read the paper, and then make everyone an early dinner. At the table, he and Charlie would argue about territorial and national issues until Ophelia stepped in and pointed out that they actually held the same opinions. Although they still argued, their relationship had also improved since Ezekiel had started his job at Belle's.

There is nothing better to unite people than a common enemy, and they had one in Luther. Ophelia once overheard them devising a plan for revenge and firmly told them never to mention his name again. On Sunday nights when Zeke was off work, he and Charlie drank together in the backyard before they both went out for the evening. Charlie played cards or hung around a faro table on Fifth Street. Ophelia had no idea where Zeke went on his night off work. Every Sunday evening she was left home alone with Nell, whom she expected to slip away at any moment.

By mid-August, temperatures climbed into the hundreds. Ophelia's attic room turned into an oven, so she laid out her bedroll and slept on the roof. Every couple of years when there was a heat spell, she'd sleep there until it broke. She wasn't ready to sleep in a bed with Charlie at night. She'd thought it might be romantic to sleep on the roof together like she'd once done with Whiskey Pete. But the fact that Charlie slept so deeply made her worry that he might roll off in the middle of the night.

One night she was on the roof laying out her bedroll and blankets, when she thought she heard voices. She crept around the side of the roof where the ledge became narrow and she could see the back garden. Both Charlie and Zeke had taken to sleeping outside because it was too hot indoors. They were still up and sat close together under the light of a hanging lantern. It looked like they were studying a map. Something about their posture, the way they sat uncharacteristically close with their heads together, roused her suspicion. She crawled through her bedroom window, bounded down the stairs, quietly exited the back door, tiptoed barefoot across the backyard, and sneaked up behind them.

"What are you two scheming?" she asked.

At the unexpected sound of her voice, they jumped, knocked their chairs over, and just about leaped out of their skins. They looked more like spooked cats than grown men. Ophelia howled with laughter.

Charlie's hand was on his revolver. "Good Lord, Ophelia. It isn't funny. I almost put a bullet in you."

Zeke and Charlie sat back down and recomposed themselves. Charlie tried to hide the paper in his hand. Zeke let out a deep sigh and took a swing from a bottle. He handed it to Charlie. They sat unusually quiet.

"I heard what you were talking about," said Ophelia.

They both took a sudden interest in their hands.

"Is there something wrong with me?" asked Ophelia.

They looked at her, at each other, and back at their hands.

"Will killing Luther fix me? Will it purify me? Will it make me a virgin again?"

An uncomfortable silence filled the dark night.

"No, it will not. It will not help me one bit. All it will do is make you feel like men, like you can protect me. But you can't. Sorry. You're ten years too late. There's nothing to be done now but forgive and forget."

Charlie and Zeke looked at each other.

"Very well. If we can't forgive, we have to forget," she said.

Ophelia was half-happy the two men she loved were bonding over something. But it couldn't be this. This would only lead to their demise. "Maybe Mormonism has been good for Luther. Maybe he's reformed. Everyone deserves a shot at redemption. Don't you agree?" she asked.

They didn't answer. They stared at the fireless firepit. Ophelia pulled up an old wooden crate, turned it over, sat, and looked around the uncouth place where they hung around, feeling a little left out of their men's activities.

Charlie finally spoke. "Ophelia, I hope you're not turning religious on us. The more I ponder existence, the more I agree with the rationalists. Anyway, if I were to listen to anything in the Bible, I'd go all the way back to the Old Testament, which, I believe, says 'an eye for an eye, a tooth for a tooth.' "

Ophelia narrowed her eyes and scowled at him. "What does that mean exactly? What are you planning on doing to him, Charlie? Are you going to rape him?"

Charlie chewed his mustache, clearly uncomfortable at the implied direction of her argument.

"Turn the other cheek. Revenge killing is wrong. It's time to cast away stones. If we have to kill someone in self-defense, that's one thing. But revenge killing is premeditated. Never mind God. Under the law, you'll hang for it. And don't talk to me about rationalism. A man of science told me when I was just seventeen years old that I was destined to be a whore because of the shape of my skull and the color of my hair. How rational is that?"

Charlie eyed her. "I don't think the color of your hair had anything to do with it. Just the shape—"

Zeke interrupted Charlie. "Why don't we just give him a good beating and leave it at that? We don't have to kill him."

Ophelia yelled, "No! I've heard enough about this. Let bygones be bygones, for God's sake!"

They were all quiet. She regretted yelling at Zeke. "How do you like working for Belle London?" she asked, trying to change the subject.

"You're working for Belle London?" Charlie asked as if it was the first he'd heard about it.

Zeke stared at him. Ophelia sighed. "Charlie, I must've told you that about a hundred times," she said.

"You have?"

"Yes!"

"Well, I must've been thinking of something else, because I didn't hear you."

"Where do you think he's been all these nights?"

"I thought he'd found a lady friend." Charlie looked at Zeke and winked.

Zeke grimaced, shook his head, and stared at the ground.

"Boy, be careful of those painted ladies," said Charlie.

Zeke glared at him and stood up. "Boy?"

"Charlie, don't call any man 'boy.' And what do you mean, be careful of those painted ladies?"

He put his hands up in a conciliatory gesture. "I apologize! I've insulted you both, and I didn't mean to. I'll just shut my trap now."

"Good night," said Zeke. He walked to his bedroll and pillow.

"Good night," said Ophelia and walked toward the house. She turned her head and smiled at Charlie, who was staring at her, probably waiting for an invitation upstairs. If only he didn't saw logs all night like a half-dead drunk, she might have invited him to sleep on the roof with her.

Two days after the incident in the backyard, Ophelia was in the kitchen with Charlie after breakfast. He finished his coffee and took out his pocket watch. "I've got to go to Salt Lake today and have this fixed. It's two minutes off from the new standardized time."

"Please, Charlie, tell me you're not caught up in this time trap. When we start counting seconds like pennies, that's it for mankind."

Charlie stared at his pocket watch. "That's the way of the world. At least the trains will run on time now."

She sighed. "Well, you don't have to go all the way to Salt

Lake, because the best watchmaker, Herman Kuchler, is right here in Ogden, a couple of doors down from the Saddle Rock. In fact, people come all the way from Salt Lake for his expertise. Take your watch to him. He can fix it as good as anyone in Salt Lake."

Charlie stood up and grabbed his hat. "He won't have the right part for this. Listen, I'd better go, or I'll miss the next train." He kissed Ophelia on the cheek and was out the back door so fast, she didn't have time to question him. She stared at the door. Something wasn't right. She hurried up to the attic and fished out her funeral dress and veil. Wiping the sweat from her brow with her forearm, she put it on as fast as she could, and ran out the door.

Disguised in widow's garb, she walked a block to a busy corner and hailed a hack to Union Station. When her carriage passed Charlie walking down the street, she slunk down so he wouldn't see her. At the station, she bought a ticket, ducked into a café, and watched from the window as Charlie waited for the train. As soon as he got onto a train car, she ran out of the café and boarded another one. In Salt Lake City, she followed him from a safe distance as he walked down Main Street.

He stopped and stood in front of the watchmaker shop, hands in his trouser pockets, contemplating it for a moment. Ophelia quickly ducked into the entryway of a bakery and peered at him from the doorway, feeling both guilty and silly. He opened the door to the watchmaker's and went in. A slip of paper fell out of his pocket and landed on the sidewalk. She scurried out of her hiding place and picked up the paper he'd dropped. An address was printed on the paper. Ophelia looked up from the paper. Charlie came out of the shop and stood before her. Like a kid caught red-handed with her hand in the candy jar, she grinned and tried to close her hand around the paper, but Charlie had already seen it.

Charlie studied her outfit. "Who died? Must be someone important if you followed me all the way here to tell me."

Ophelia sighed and looked at him. The whole time she thought he had no idea she was there. It occurred to her now that he knew all along. "How long have you known I was following you?"

"I noticed you at the station." He held out his hand for the paper.

"Did you drop this paper on purpose to bait me?" She held her chin up in defiance, uncurled her hand, and stared at the address, saying it out loud so she'd remember it. She gave the paper back to Charlie and started walking in the direction of the address written on the paper, repeating it to herself so she wouldn't forget.

Charlie didn't try to stop her. "It's quite a few blocks." He called to her back. "Do you want to take a hack?" Ophelia kept walking and didn't reply. He fell into step behind her. They walked in silence.

The address led to an impressive yet innocent-looking three-story house with a porch surrounded by pink rose hedges. She stared, her jaw set and her body tense. Someone was inside. Was it him? The blood pounded in her head and her heart thumped. Part of her wanted to turn around and get the hell out of there; another part was fired up for battle. Curtains from a second-floor window moved. Ophelia opened the gate, walked up the stairs, and stood on the porch. Charlie followed. They stared at the lion's mouth of a brass knocker. Neither of them moved. Finally, Ophelia extended her arm and reached toward it.

Charlie said, "You don't have to—"

She knocked with a trembling yet determined hand. Less than three seconds later, a young redheaded girl, who looked to be about sixteen, cracked opened the door and studied them. Because she'd opened the door so fast, Ophelia guessed she'd known they were there, and that she'd been the person watching from the second-floor window. The young girl opened the door wider. They stared at her bulging womb. An older woman pulled her away from the door, closed it a little, and scolded her.

"Martha, you know that you're not allowed to answer the door. It's too dangerous. Now stay in the kitchen and finish your chores." She popped her head out the partially opened door. "May I help you?"

It was the Widow Hopkins. She looked closer at Ophelia, opened the door all the way, then covered her mouth with her hands, dropped them to her sides, and reached out to embrace her. "Ophelia Oatman!" She squeezed Ophelia. It wasn't a cordial social embrace. It was a giant bear hug that nearly crushed her bones. "Why, Sister Ophelia, I thought I'd never see you again."

She finally let go, held Ophelia at arm's length, and looked her over closely. "Sister Thompson sent word that you'd passed through Grafton. But no one really believed her." She paused. "Why, you're all in black. Did someone pass, dear? Are you a widow? Who is this gentleman here? Where have you been all these years? We've been looking for you. Oh, I apologize. Too many questions!" She looked behind her to where the young girl had disappeared. "I'm sorry you had to hear that. It's just, since the Edmunds Act, they've been arresting our men and breaking up families. It's awful. We have to protect our family. Your Uncle Luther would be thrilled to see you. Did Sister Thompson tell you that he and I are married now? That makes me your aunt!"

Ophelia nodded.

"Unfortunately, he's away until Thursday." She looked behind her into the house. "And I have the Relief Society in my parlor right now. I hate to ask you this, but can you come back

Thursday at this same time or thereabouts?" She wore a pained, apologetic expression.

Ophelia stood dumbfounded. One minute she was being taken in and the next turned away. "Of course. I'm sorry to intrude."

"Intrude? Oh, no, not at all. You're welcome any time. How long—" High-pitched ladies' voices erupted from inside the house. The Widow Hopkins turned her head toward them and back to Ophelia nervously. "Oh, dear, any time—except now. We'll talk on Thursday. Will that be all right? Luther will be so pleased."

Ophelia and Charlie walked slowly back to the train station. "Charlie, did you see that young girl?"

"Of course, I saw her. She looks like a younger version of you. It's clear what motivated Luther's conversion to Mormonism."

Ophelia's disgust and hatred for Luther intensified, but she didn't want to give Charlie any more provocation for vengeance, so she said nothing more. Somehow Luther had infiltrated the inner circle of Mormon power. She wouldn't return on Thursday or any other day. If he found her and Zeke, there'd be serious trouble. He could reignite his allegations that Zeke had been a traitor during the Black Hawk War, and government officials could hang him for that. And Luther could try again to take the ruby necklace. She'd rather die than give it to him. The best thing to do was sell the house and get out of town as quickly as possible.

Charlie gave her a nudge and a sly smile. "Polygamy is illegal now, even in the territories. We could turn them into the federal agents. Then we'd have revenge with no violence."

Ophelia entertained the idea for a minute. "No, Charlie. That's just the Mormon way. Polygamy is part of their religion, and one of the reasons they came all the way out here to Utah.

Besides, if Luther went to jail, what would happen to Widow Hopkins and that poor young girl with child?"

Twelve

Between Monday and Thursday Ophelia changed her mind several times about whether or not she would face her demon and meet with Luther. Part of her knew she should take the high road, play it safe, and not wake a sleeping beast. Another part of her wanted to show that he couldn't destroy her so easily; despite the damage he'd done, she was wealthy, in love, and, most importantly, she still possessed the ruby necklace.

On Thursday morning, instead of dressing conservatively in a restrictive corset and bustle, she slipped on a comfortable and somewhat scandalous rational-style dress: light and flowing with a delicate rose print, fashionable in Paris but not Utah. She pinned her hair in a loose bun and looked in the full-length mirror. From the bed, Dolly stared at her with her one remaining black eye. Ophelia picked up Dolly, stuck her fingers into the small slit on her back, and retrieved the hidden necklace. Her fingertips felt a pulse in the necklace as if it were living. She both loved and despised the necklace.

She wanted to know its secrets. She wanted to know if her uncle's claim that her mother had stolen it was true. If her mother had stolen it, there had to have been a good reason. Although her mother had become pregnant with Ezekiel out of wedlock, she was still a good and honest person, and she wouldn't have stolen something unless she'd had a valid reason.

Ophelia stood close to the mirror and fastened the necklace. The red rubies complimented the roses on her dress. Her whole appearance, especially the necklace, was a nose-thumb at Luther. She'd look him in the eye, keep her head high, and torment him with the ruby necklace he so desperately wanted.

A shadow of doubt overtook her, and she wondered if she should change her clothes. She poked through her overstuffed armoire full of expensive dresses for every occasion, most of which had belonged to Pearl, who had believed that, if a whore wore a prim dress, she'd cease to be a whore. Ophelia put her hand on one of Pearl's favorite dresses and closed her eyes, calling on Pearl's spirit to give her strength. She'd been the only woman Ophelia had ever known who had stood her ground in front of intimidating men. The only man she ever cowered from was Johnny Dobbs, and that was only because he aimed to kill her. Even though Pearl had lacked physical strength and seemed uncomfortable with animals and the land, she'd possessed some peculiar quality that made her a powerful force of nature.

Next to a hatbox on the floor were Red Farrell's boots. She slid into them. Of course, she had to wear them; they were symbols of her guilt-stained courage. In Frisco, Zeke had teased her and told her to get rid of them. Yet they seemed to have a life of their own, and she'd been unable to throw them out. Like the ruby necklace, they seemed to possess her, rather than she possessing them. The boots' red-embossed cuffs matched the red roses and ruby necklace. So what if they looked mannish and strange. They made a statement. She wished there was a way to transfer Red Farrell's ghost from her to Luther, because she knew Red would hate and torment him. But Red usually only showed up when she was alone.

Ophelia wanted to rid herself of the young girl who'd been violated by her uncle and then shot him and run away. After all she'd been through over the past decade, a man like Luther certainly couldn't hurt her. Yet the scraggly group of men in Frisco had turned her into a quivering bowl of pudding. This time she'd be strong. She'd meet with Luther, show off the necklace, snub her nose at him, sell the house, and run off to Paris where it was acceptable to dress in a comfortable Bohemian style and follow one's passions.

She descended the creaky stairs and crept down the hall to Charlie's room, where she stopped, rested her head on the door jamb, and watched as he sat on the bed inspecting his six-shooter.

She whispered from the doorway. "Charlie, do you have to bring that today? You might be tempted, especially if trouble arises."

He jumped. "Sweet Jesus, Ophelia. You've got to stop sneaking up on me." He shook his head and placed the gun in his holster under his jacket. "That's exactly why I carry it—in case trouble arises. And that's why every morning I check that the chambers are full." He grinned at her. "Why are you hovering there? Come on in here. You haven't given me a single kiss in about a week now."

Ophelia walked into the room and stood in front of him, feeling shy and uncertain, mostly about her outfit.

"You look beautiful. But maybe—" he paused and stared at the necklace.

"Maybe what, Charlie?"

He shook his head and patted the pearl handle of his revolver. "It's a good thing Colt's coming."

"Charlie, I'm not going to cause trouble. I bet Widow Hopkins and the Mormons have reformed Luther into a Saint. That's what they do. So good. We'll see to that, and then we can finally forget the bastard and live in peace."

Charlie nodded in agreement. "I don't intend to cause trouble. That necklace, however, just might provoke him. Are you sure you want to wear it?"

Ophelia plopped in a chair and touched the necklace around

her throat. Maybe he was right. Anger rose and burned in her belly. No. He'd raped her. He'd ruined her for marriage and made her what she was. "Yes, I'm sure."

Charlie looked down, pointed at her boots, and smirked. "Okay, you do look real nice, but you're wearing those boots again! Didn't you say you were going to get rid of those after Frisco?"

Ophelia stood, put her hands on her hips, looked down at the boots, and grinned back at him. "Yes. I did say that, didn't I? It's the strangest thing." She shook her head. "I just can't bear to part with them. Don't mention them to Ezekiel, please. There's only so much teasing a girl can take."

Charlie studied her closer. "The boots make an odd match with the dress. But you still look pretty to me." He grabbed her by the wrist and pulled her onto his lap.

Ophelia held Charlie's face in her hands. "Charlie, when we get back, promise me you'll convince Zeke to drop the revenge plan on Luther so we can live in peace."

"And then you'll marry me?"

"We're together. Isn't that all that matters? Why should we care about marriage?"

Ophelia waited for his response. She could tell he was being careful with his words so he wouldn't offend her. She smiled and poked him in the chest. "You can't make an honest woman out of me, Charlie. That's what was on the tip of your tongue, wasn't it?" She hopped off his lap. "See? There's no good reason for us to marry."

"No. That's what you said, not me. Those are your words. Maybe my reasons are beyond reason." He sighed and looked at his pocket watch. "If we're going to make the train, we'd better get moving."

Thirteen

Ophelia watched from the train window as farms and factories rushed past. The wild land between Ogden and the Great Salt Lake Valley had been cultivated. Barbed-wire fences crossed all the fields where wild herds had once roamed. She saw ravens picking at the carcass of a dead animal entangled in a fence.

A feeling of panic and dread came over her, and she reached over to Charlie in the seat next to her and grabbed his arm. "Good God, what the hell are we doing?"

"We're going to meet the swine known as your uncle, Luther, so as you can convince me I shouldn't kill him. That's the purpose of our journey today, isn't it? To see how a man can be reformed, to let go of revenge and let justice lie in the hands of something or someone greater than us?"

Ophelia whispered, "And if you find him unreformed, reprehensible, and utterly repugnant, will you take up arms against him? Or let bygones be bygones."

"Your wish is my command."

"I just want peace, Charlie. That is my wish." She looked at him, and he met her look. Then his gaze fell to the ruby necklace, and she knew what he was thinking. It felt heavy around her neck. She closed her eyes.

They walked east six blocks from the train depot to Luther's house with the sun glaring in their faces. They reached his house. Ophelia looked up and noticed movement from the second-story window. She hesitated and thought about turning around, but her skin was burning and the shady porch offered refuge, so she climbed the stairs, stood in the shade, and felt the heat drain from her face.

Charlie stood next to her and waited. “You don’t have to do this,” he said.

The house itself looked innocent and homey: rose bushes, fruit trees, a white fence, even a swing in the corner of the porch. What demons could possibly live in such an innocent oasis? Poor Widow Hopkins probably had no idea she’d married a monster.

Charlie and Ophelia stared at the gaping mouth of the gilded lion door-knocker. Neither of them moved. Finally Charlie reached out. Before he even touched the lion, the door opened, and the pregnant red-haired girl, who was forbidden to answer it, peered out. Someone pulled her from behind and tried to shut the door. Charlie and Ophelia exchanged glances as the muffled sounds of a scuffle took place behind the partially closed door.

Flustered, Widow Hopkins finally pulled the door open. Ophelia had known her for so long as Widow Hopkins. She couldn’t think of her by another name, especially not Aunt.

“Welcome! You’ll have to excuse that girl. She is the sacred vessel for the newest member of our family, but she’s as dull and stubborn as a mule. We can’t risk letting her answer the door. Impending statehood and federal control threaten our most cherished beliefs. But how rude of me to talk politics! Do come in! You must be dying in this heat. Luther is waiting for you in the parlor.” She ushered them into the foyer. “I’ve made fresh lemonade and scones. Ophelia, do you remember back in Grafton when a lemon was so dear?”

“I remember you talked about lemons, but in all honesty, I’d never actually seen one until I was much older.”

“Oh, my laws! Life has improved. Thank the Lord for that.

Luther was so thrilled to hear you're alive and right here in the Great Salt Lake Valley. Dear, we thought you were dead, or lost to us forever. If it's not too much of a strain, you must tell us the whole story of your kidnapping."

Charlie and Ophelia exchanged glances again. They followed Widow Hopkins through open French doors into the parlor where Luther sat. He rose from his chair and started toward them. Ophelia had forgotten his height and presence. As he moved toward her, heat emanated from his large body. She fought the urge to run out of the house. He saw the ruby necklace and was unable to shift his gaze. Although he smiled, Ophelia saw the murderous look in his eyes and realized she'd made a grave mistake. He grabbed her by the shoulders and squeezed her in a phony gesture of affection. His fingers dug into her flesh so hard that after he removed his hands, she could still feel his touch.

"Ophelia, my dearest niece, I'm so relieved you're safe and well. I searched for you for so many years. It's hard to imagine what that scoundrel must have done to you, and how you escaped and survived." He shook his head in contrived indignation.

The Widow Hopkins consoled him and patted his arm "There, there, dear. Let's not get angry. This is a happy occasion."

The stifling room closed around Ophelia, and her cheeks felt as if they were on fire. Maybe the sun had burned them on the walk from the train station, or maybe the blaze came from being in the same room as her uncle. It was too late to escape. Luther took a kerchief from his pocket, wiped his brow, and rolled his fat tongue over his lips in the same sickening manner he'd always done.

Feeling weak, Ophelia looked at the Widow and wondered, how could she tolerate this man?

Luther extended his hand to Charlie and introduced himself, "Luther Cashman. Pleased to meet you," he said.

Cashman? Ophelia had never known her mother's maiden name, never heard it spoken, never seen it written. Charlie nodded, but didn't extend his hand or introduce himself. Ophelia couldn't speak. An awkward silence filled the room.

"And are you my niece's husband?" Luther asked.

His niece? How dare he claim possession of her? She wasn't his anything.

Charlie snapped out of his silent trance. He recognized where he was and who he was talking to, yet still made no motion to shake Luther's hand. "No, not husband. Prospective fiancé—Char—ah, Green, Thomas Green."

Luther dropped his hand, nodded, and turned to Ophelia. She didn't want him to touch her again. She'd die if he touched her again. As he came toward her, she stepped closer to Charlie.

With his large hairy hands, still laden with gaudy rings, he again squeezed her shoulders, dug his fingers in, and smiled as he stared at the necklace. "Ophelia, I'm relieved to see you alive and unharmed." Sweat formed on his brow. The pressure of his fingers was unbearable. Charlie looked at the hands on her shoulders and glared at Luther with visible distaste. He seemed about to say something when Widow Hopkins spoke.

"Oh, Luther, come now, they must be tired and thirsty. It's so hot. Everyone, have a seat and let's have some refreshment." She ushered them into uncomfortable parlor chairs, and once they were all seated, rang a bell. A few minutes later, the red-haired girl emerged, balancing a tray with a pitcher of lemonade and a plate of scones on her bulging belly. No one spoke as she placed the tray on a sideboard. "Thank you, Martha," said Widow Hopkins.

The girl didn't make a sound but stared at Ophelia as she exited. Perhaps she was mute. Widow Hopkins stood, poured glasses of lemonade, and handed one to each of them.

When she handed Ophelia her lemonade, she noticed the necklace. "Ophelia, that's a beautiful necklace! Do you mind if I take a closer look?"

"Of course not," said Ophelia. She formed a small defiant smile, but still couldn't bring herself to look at Luther.

Widow Hopkins bent over and peered at the necklace.

Luther couldn't sit still. His anger was palpable, almost tangible. She had awakened a beast. He still pined for the ruby necklace. It couldn't be merely the money the necklace might fetch. He appeared affluent. Why would the necklace have such a hold on him? Ophelia watched Charlie watch Luther as Widow Hopkins inspected the necklace.

"This is absolutely exquisite!" declared Widow Hopkins. "Was it a gift from you, Mr. Green?"

Charlie looked from Widow Hopkins to Ophelia and paused. "Uh—"

Before Charlie could begin his nervous habit of chewing his mustache, Ophelia answered for him. "No, it belonged to *my* mother."

"It belonged to my mother!" Luther erupted. He stood, walked to the sidebar, and poured himself another glass of lemonade, which he downed in one gulp and then slammed on the table. Widow Hopkins looked hurt by his outburst and lack of manners.

Ophelia finally dared to look at him "Yes. And your mother gave it to my mother, who gave it to me as she lay dying."

Luther pointed an accusing finger at Ophelia. "My mother gave her nothing. After she disgraced herself and the family, she was disowned. Your mother stole that necklace!" He turned to his wife. "That necklace belongs around your neck because it rightfully belongs to me."

Widow Hopkins's mouth hung open and she clutched her throat.

The room fell silent.

Ophelia finally spoke. "Why would mother's family disown her because she was violated by an Indian? That wasn't her fault."

"Violated!" Luther snickered. "She was far from violated. Certain types of women find heathens alluring. They don't have the morality or will power to resist temptation and control their lust, so they meet with the savage willingly, and then claim violation."

Charlie set his lemonade on a side table and began to rise from his seat. Ophelia froze. The way Luther had spoken about her dead mother made her wish she'd never tried to stop Ezekiel and Charlie from killing him.

Widow Hopkins tried to smooth the contention. She placed her hands on her hips and addressed them all as if they were children. "Luther! I don't give a hoot about owning that necklace. It looks beautiful on Ophelia. At my age, wearing such jewels would only invite scorn and ridicule. Now, please, this is not a subject for polite conversation."

Luther ran his hand through his hair and then rubbed his face with his hands as if he were putting on a mask. "As usual, you're absolutely right. It's not a subject for polite conversation. I'm sorry, cherished wife, if I upset you." He shot Ophelia a disingenuous, conciliatory smile and turned to Widow Hopkins. "My dear wife, please show Ophelia the garden while I have a man-to-man chat with Mr. Green. If he and Ophelia are to be wed, there are matters we must discuss." He stood up and shooed them outside like dogs, "Run along now. When I was in the garden this morning, I noticed the peaches are ripe. Take Ophelia and pick her a basket of peaches for the road."

The way he emphasized the word *peaches* roused Ophelia's

suspicion. Did he know about her former alias as Miss Peach? If so, then he probably knew she lived in Ogden. She should've let Charlie and Ezekiel kill him. Now he had the upper hand and could ruin her all over again, just when her fortunes had changed.

Widow Hopkins smiled and nodded. "Wonderful idea. The fresh air will do us good. Now, no more arguing about family heirlooms. Jewelry doesn't matter. What matters is that Ophelia is safe, and you've been reunited."

"Words of wisdom from the wife, as usual." Luther put his hand on Charlie's shoulder in a chummy manner and led him out of the room into an adjoining study. Ophelia watched him take Charlie away. She burned with anger, suspicion, and a deep, familiar fear she hadn't felt in a long time. Luther smiled a slick snaky grin and closed the study door. Widow Hopkins beamed at the closed door. How could she have fallen for a man like that? The door clicked shut, and Ophelia froze. Widow Hopkins touched her elbow and gently led her through the house to the backyard.

Fourteen

The backyard had a fairy-tale quality: honeysuckle and fruit trees, roses of every color, and more cherubic statues than Ophelia could possibly count. Words poured from Widow Hopkins's mouth, but Ophelia was too shaken to make sense of them. Widow Hopkins could have been speaking Chinese. She couldn't follow her idle small talk, while Luther had Charlie in his grip.

What if Charlie got mad and killed him? Charlie had an even temper now but as a young man, he'd killed his sister's rapist and almost killed another man in a fight. Leaving him alone in a room with Luther was dangerous. But surely he was too smart to kill Luther in his own house in broad daylight with his wife in the garden.

Widow Hopkins clucked her tongue and shook her head. "And of all the nerve, that boy, that Godless horse thief, blamed you for shooting Luther. Can you imagine? Well, of course, we didn't believe him—"

Ophelia stared at Widow Hopkins in disbelief. "What? Pardon me? What boy? What did he say? I'm sorry. I don't understand. Can you repeat what you were saying?"

"Oh, dear. It must be quite upsetting for you to be reminded of all this. Excuse my insensitivity. If you prefer, we don't have to discuss this now. But someday—"

"Please excuse me. I wasn't listening. I was preoccupied with something else. What were you saying about the horse thief and shooting Uncle Luther?"

"Oh, what was that boy's name? Cah—Cahoon? No, that's not it. It rhymes with sox, oh yes, Cox! When we caught him, he had the nerve to tell us it was all your idea, shooting poor Luther, stealing the money, and then running off together. Can you imagine? He swore he didn't kill or violate you. They gave him a good working over, and he led them out to the middle of the desert into a deep rocky maze where he told them you'd fallen from a cliff. Of course, they never found you or your body. They were all set to hang him. But somehow he broke free. And they never found him. A couple of the men almost died out there, searching the desert for him. You see; we do look after our own. You were one of us, Ophelia. *Are* one of us or, if you aren't now, you could be again." Widow Hopkins grabbed Ophelia's hand, looked behind her shoulder, and then back at her. She spoke earnestly in a low voice that conveyed urgency. "Listen, there could be serious trouble if you don't cooperate. Luther seems to believe the boy's story. He thinks you shot him."

Ophelia was silent. She didn't smile, or nod, or even flinch, so as not to encourage Widow Hopkins. "And what do you believe?"

The older woman looked confused and a bit shocked, as if no one had ever asked her opinion. "First of all, I'm not Widow Hopkins anymore. You can call me Aunt May now. Second, I don't know what to believe. There's all kinds of gossip floating around. Please tell me what really happened."

Ophelia hesitated and didn't respond.

"Well, I can tell this is bringing back bad memories." Widow Hopkins patted Ophelia's hand. "You don't have to talk about it. I know the types of things an outlaw might do to a young girl. Listen, you may be soiled by your unfortunate past, but at least you still have your looks and a good mind, which is very important. You were one of the best readers on the settlement, adults included. Remember my secret trunk of books? Never underestimate the importance of intelligence. Luther and I have learned that firsthand, thanks to Martha. She's such a dunce!" Widow Hopkins winced, as if the mention of the girl caused her physical pain. "I pray every day our child doesn't turn out to be a moron like her blood mother."

Widow Hopkins looked at her for some kind of response, but Ophelia remained still and silent, afraid if she moved or spoke, something inside her would burst.

"Does Mr. Green know of your past? If not, I'd keep it a secret. No need for him to know he's getting damaged goods."

Ophelia put one hand against her forehead, and with the other, she held her stomach. "I'm sorry. I feel very unwell. The bad memories and the heat must've made me ill. May I use your privy?"

"Of course. Follow the path to the back of the garden, and you'll find it there next to a rosebush. Soon we'll have a water closet inside." Widow Hopkins looked at Ophelia with pity and regret. "I'm so sorry. I shouldn't have pressed you. First Luther's rude behavior, and then I drag up the past. Do forgive us."

Ophelia walked through the garden toward the privy with her heart racing, barely able to breathe, feeling like she had to get out of there or she'd die. She tried to compose herself and returned to a shady spot in the garden where Widow Hopkins sat with a sympathetic smile glued to her face. She told Widow Hopkins that she was sick and must end her visit.

Widow Hopkins begged Ophelia to stay and lie down in one of their beds, but she refused. She couldn't wait to get out of there. She never wanted to see either Luther or Widow Hopkins again. She felt terrible for the girl, Martha, the second wife, the poor pregnant idiot, who would soon bear their child.

Ophelia and Widow Hopkins entered the parlor as Martha was drinking the leftover lemonade. "I'll just pop in to the study and let them know you're not feeling well," said Widow Hopkins.

As soon as Widow Hopkins left the room, Martha grabbed Ophelia's hand, pressed a folded paper into it, and scurried back to the kitchen. Ophelia watched the girl with confused pity and kept her hand closed around the paper.

Widow Hopkins emerged from the study, followed by Luther and Charlie. Luther patted him on the shoulder and chuckled deeply, as if they were old chums. Charlie grinned. Ophelia felt betrayed as he laughed at something Luther had said. What could possibly be so funny?

"Ophelia, you look very pale. Maybe you should sit down," said Widow Hopkins.

The men stopped laughing. An exaggerated look of concern spread over Luther's face. No one else seemed to recognize he was a phony. Charlie wore the slack expression of a man who'd just taken a few too many shots of liquor. Ophelia narrowed her eyes and studied Charlie's demeanor for clues about what had transpired in the study.

"I'm feeling dreadful. I'm afraid we must go," she said, directing her comment at Charlie.

"Oh, what a pity! Dearest Ophelia, we have so much to talk about. When will you visit us again?" asked Luther.

"Uh, I don't know. But we must go now. I certainly don't want to spread my illness to anyone else," said Ophelia.

Charlie made no motion to leave.

"Please, Charlie," Ophelia whispered.

He moved toward the hat rack.

Luther struck a thoughtful pose. "Wait a minute. Where are your peaches, Ophelia? You can't possibly leave without at least a few of our delicious peaches. Dearest wife, please take Mr. Green to the back garden and show him the peach tree. There's a small box near the back door you can use, so they won't get bruised in transport."

"Oh, I love peaches," said Charlie. He turned toward Widow Hopkins. Ophelia began to protest, but it was too late. Widow Hopkins and Charlie were on their way out to the garden, and Ophelia was alone with Luther.

When they were out of sight, he moved to her, grabbed her arms, and shook her.

"You will give me that necklace, or I will make your life a living hell."

Ophelia winced. "Let go of me, or I will tell your adoring wife what you did to me."

"Ha! What did I do to you? I did nothing to you. Why you're a whore and a thief. You shot me. That young cowhand was almost hanged because of you! No one will believe a word you say, Miss Peach."

"You're a damned hypocrite," Ophelia hissed.

"That's right, talk like a whore." He squeezed her chin, tilted her head back, and looked down into her eyes. "You dirty Jezebel." He let go and glared at her with disgust. "How much do you charge anyway?"

"You ruined me. What I became is your fault."

"I accelerated the inevitable. You're a bad seed, just like your mother."

Her hands trembled and her whole body shook with rage. If Charlie's six-shooter had been in reach, she would have shot Luther herself. He grabbed her by the neck and tried to unclasp the necklace. With the point of Red's old boot, she kicked him as hard as she could in the shin. He cursed, removed his hands from around her neck, rubbed his leg, and stared at the boots with pain and wonder.

He began to lurch at her again, but must've heard Widow Hopkins and Charlie coming, because he straightened into a normal posture, smiled tightly, and ran his fingers through his hair, which, despite his age, was still thick and dark, and as tangled as a pit of vipers. He looked like the demon he was. Why had her mother written to him for help? Luther hated her mother with ferocious intensity.

Martha came in and placed the plate of uneaten scones on a tray. As she passed by, Widow Hopkins grabbed the plate from the tray and held it under Charlie and Ophelia's noses. "Oh, but you haven't had one of my delicious scones. Won't you just stay a little longer and taste one?"

Ophelia put her hand on her stomach. "I'm feeling very ill."

"It may settle your stomach."

Charlie stood next to Widow Hopkins and stared at the scones with desire. Widow Hopkins handed the plate back to Martha. When Widow Hopkins turned away, Charlie quickly swiped one and placed it in the basket with the peaches. Ophelia gave Charlie a disapproving look and motioned with her head toward the front door.

Widow Hopkins fetched their hats from the hat rack. "Where are you staying? Will you come again before you head back to California? Ophelia, if the retelling isn't too hard for you, I'd really like to hear your story. Did you know that your cousins on your father's side were kidnapped by Apaches in Arizona? Why, the kidnapping of Oatman girls is almost an epidemic!"

Ophelia was close to the door, almost free, but curiosity got the best of her. "What cousins? I never heard that story. I didn't know I had cousins."

"Oh, yes, they were Mormons too, but they were Josephites, and they decided to take the southern route to California on the Old Spanish Trail. The rescue party pieced the bones together, and everyone was accounted for except the girls. They figured the Apaches kidnapped and sold them. They were known for doing that."

Bewildered, Ophelia stared at Widow Hopkins. "I didn't even know I had cousins," she said.

"Come back and visit when you feel better. There's more I can tell you."

Charlie and Luther had become engaged in conversation. "Do you know anything about my mother's family?" she whispered to Widow Hopkins.

"Why, no! I've never heard Luther speak of your mother at all until today. I apologize he was so rude, he—" Widow Hopkins realized Luther and Charlie had stopped talking and were listening, so she dropped the topic. "Thank you so much for coming."

As soon as the front door shut behind them, Ophelia ran down the steps and nearly tripped. The secret note from Martha was still clenched in her hand and had become damp with her perspiration. She unfolded the paper, and read, *help me,* neatly written but with the P formed backward.

The afternoon heat shimmered above the road, and the dry air baked her nostrils. Ophelia stopped and wiped perspiration from her face. Even though he was drunk, Charlie noticed her discomfort.

"It's hot and you don't feel well. Should we take a carriage?" He held the basket of peaches under one arm and with his free hand lifted the scone to his mouth. Ophelia stopped walking and glared at him.

He stopped, too, looked at the scone, and then held it out to her. "Would you like some? Might make you feel better."

"No, thank you. I'm not really sick, Charlie. I just wanted to get the hell out of there. I'd like to walk even though it's hot, because I'm so angry my whole body feels like it's going to explode." She detected a subtle change in him and wondered what lie Luther had told him that had poisoned him against her.

"I'm starving. I haven't eaten all day," he said and shoved the scone into his mouth. Some crumbs fell to the ground and others clung to his mustache.

"Charlie, why were you laughing when you came out of the study with Luther? What did he say to you?"

"I'm sorry. As depraved as he may be, he's a funny man. I wanted to hate him. I was ready to put a bullet in him with my old Colt .45 here. But somehow he—I don't know. He dissolved my anger with his humor and hospitality."

Ophelia sniffed liquor and noticed the slovenly way Charlie was eating the scone. "I'm sure the liquor also helped."

Charlie stopped walking and looked at Ophelia like a guilty kid. "How did you know?"

"Please. I might not be a crack-shot private investigator, but I do own a nose." She rolled her eyes. "I'm surprised Widow Hopkins puts up with it. He's a hypocrite and a charlatan."

"Yes, but also funny," said Charlie as he stuffed the last of the scone into his mouth.

"Funny?" she shook her head and shot Charlie a hurt look, which he didn't register because he was half-cocked, completely focused on the scone, and oblivious to the horrific experience Ophelia had endured on their seemingly cordial visit. She had expected to have to defend Luther from Charlie's wrath, but instead Charlie had gotten drunk and fallen under Luther's spell.

As they resumed walking, her right leg began to ache from the old, never-fully-healed injury she'd incurred when she fell off the cliff in the desert. Charlie walked beside her with the basket of peaches under his arm. He had a slight limp as well. She didn't know why. Maybe because of the booze; maybe he had an old injury, too. He'd never told her that story.

Despite his ever-present Colt, he now seemed like a boy who needed protection. Was it because he'd fallen for Luther, or because of the childish way he'd just stuffed the scone into his mouth? Maybe it was the basket of fruit under his arm. Ophelia struggled to hold her tongue and suppress the murderous rage she felt toward Luther. If she said what she felt, Charlie would think her insane. Instead of speaking her mind, she smiled and joked. "Look at the two of us limping."

"Let's sit in the shade and enjoy a peach," he said.

"Even if I were starving to death, I wouldn't eat one of those peaches," she said.

"Well, he never actually touched them. I picked them straight from the tree. And the tree never did anything bad to anyone."

Fifteen

On the train ride back to Ogden, many passengers sought relief from the heat and opened their windows. Newspapers, hats, hairstyles, and everything else that wasn't tied down were blown about in the horizontal tornado resulting from the cross breeze. The passengers finally succumbed to the wind, held tightly to their belongings, and rooted themselves like trees in their seats.

Ophelia took off her hat and held it tightly on her lap. Charlie's head drooped and bobbed in deep sleep to the rhythm of the train's movement. Ophelia eyed him, disappointed that a man could be swayed so easily by liquor.

It had taken six weeks or so, but they'd all settled into a peaceful life in Ogden. Although she worried about Zeke's employment at Belle London's brothel, at least he was occupied and not addicted to opium. If Luther knew Ophelia had been Miss Peach, then he knew they lived in Ogden and not California. What else did he know? Did he know Ezekiel was living in Ogden with her?

She decided to put the house up for sale immediately, before something bad happened. She wanted to go as far away as she could, maybe all the way to the coast, maybe to Paris. Somewhere Luther'd never find her. His touch had marked her, and she couldn't erase his burning afterimage. She needed to take a long bath or jump in a freezing lake or the ocean to fully cleanse all traces of him.

When the train pulled into the Ogden depot, Ophelia elbowed

Charlie. He didn't waken, and for a fleeting moment, she imagined Luther had poisoned him. She shook him a little too hard, and he jumped, startled and confused, until he fully woke up and realized they'd arrived and he'd been asleep. Although it was nearly six, the summer sun still blazed on the northwest horizon.

The one scone hadn't satisfied Charlie's hunger, and he suggested they stop at the Saddle Rock Restaurant for supper. Ophelia hadn't eaten all day. Hunger mixed with anxiety had tied her stomach into a knot, and she didn't know if she could eat. But she agreed anyway, hoping that over dinner Charlie would tell her what Luther had said to him in the study.

They stopped at a bench on their way between the station and the Saddle Rock. She patted her hair and attempted to tuck it under her hat. "I'd like to eat at the Saddle Rock. But Charlie, look at my hair. I look like the Wild Boy from Aveyron. I can barely put my hat on with it sticking up like this."

Charlie assessed her hair, placed the box of peaches on the bench, licked the palm of his hand, and patted down some loose strands. "Maybe I can help you fix it. Remember I had a sister once. After our mother died, she taught me how to braid her hair."

Ophelia rummaged through her disheveled hair, pulled out a few hairpins, and handed them to him. She placed her hat down, wound up her hair, and held it in place. "See what you can do," she said with little faith.

He put the two hairpins in his mouth and used both hands. His determined look reminded Ophelia of her father. Although she had never witnessed her father arrange a woman's hair, he'd had the same determined look whenever he concentrated on repairing something. Her eyes welled with tears at Charlie's tenderness and the memory of her father.

Charlie finished, stepped back, assessed his work, and looked satisfied with the result. He noticed Ophelia's tears. "What's the matter? Did I hurt you?"

"Luther is a bad man, Charlie. He's a very bad man."

Charlie took a clean hankie from his pocket and dabbed her tears. "Well, all right. It's all right. He won't hurt you. I'll see to that. Now, let's go get something to eat. I think you could use a drink. It's been a long hot day. Come on now, don't cry."

They walked a block to the Saddle Rock Restaurant. A banner over the doorway advertised *Oyster in Every Style,* and an Oriental gentleman dressed in western attire showed them to a corner table near an open window. She stared at the electric ceiling fan, grateful for the breeze and amazed at the invention. In addition to the fan, the Chinese restaurant's proprietors had also installed a water closet, hoping to attract the high-class customers who traveled by rail and were accustomed to such amenities in large cities like New York and Boston.

The waiter came for their order. "We have oyster in every style," he reminded them and read from a paper in his hand. "Blue Points, Saddle Wocks, Wockaways, Lynnhavens, Cape Cods, Buzzard Bays, Cotuits, Shewsburys." He took a breath and looked at them. "Fwied oysters, oyster pie, oyster patties, oyster box stew, oyster pompadour, Algonquin, à la Newburg, à la Nethalan, à la poulette." He took a breath and glanced at them again.

Charlie tried to say something, but he was too slow, and the waiter continued.

"Oysters woasted on toast, broiled in shell, served with cocktail sauce, stewed in milk or cream, fwied with bacon, escalloped, fwicasseed, pickled, waw on the half shell, angels on horseback, hangtown fwy?"

They both grinned. "Did you get all that?" Charlie asked Ophelia. He addressed the waiter. "We'll start with two glasses of ale and oysters on the half shell." The waiter nodded and walked away. A few minutes later he set two glasses of ale on the table.

Ophelia picked up her glass and held it to her cheek. "Oh, my, it's cold."

"They built a small ice house in the basement," said Charlie.

"Incredible. Wait a minute. How do you know what's in the basement?"

Charlie smiled. "There's also a faro table and a weekly poker game down there."

Ophelia nodded and took another sip of the cold ale. "Oh, so you're a regular. That explains where you've been going every Sunday night. Well, a gambling den is better than the brothel."

Charlie smirked. "I'm all yours now. No more brothels for me."

After a few sips of ale Ophelia excused herself and went to visit the water closet. She splashed cool water on her face from a pipe over the basin and glanced in the mirror. Her hair was still all out of place, but she decided not to bother with it. The cold ale had relaxed her. In the hallway on her way back to the table, a man stepped in front of her and blocked the way.

Annoyed, she said, "Excuse me," in an exaggerated tone. She looked at the man's face. It was Whiskey Pete, the distillery operating jack Mormon who'd once been her beau. Ophelia hadn't seen him since the Christmas Eve he'd decided to repent and had shown up on her doorstop with a knife-wielding *avenging angel* from the Mormon Church. Whiskey Pete's face was sheepish, apologetic, and pleading.

Ophelia gave him a cold look. "I have nothing to say to you. Get out of my way."

"Oh Peeeaacch, please," he purred. "Forgive me." He took a step toward her.

Ophelia took a step back and looked over his shoulder to see if Charlie could see them.

She spoke in a low, harsh whisper so no one else would hear, but it was difficult to control her anger. "You had no right to come to my house on Christmas Eve with that horrible bishop and treat me that way. Pearl had just died. I was all alone in the world. You are a bastard. Get out of my way."

"I'm so sorry Peach. I should never have done that to you." He shook his head and looked at the floor. "I got excommunicated anyway. Now I'm an apostate, a son of purrrdition." He stepped closer and spoke in a confessional tone. She smelled liquor on his breath. "I lost my second wife, poor little sparrow. She died giving birth to a ten-pound ox. But at least I have a son now—big boy. Too bad he had to be born so big to a gal so small. Funny, because my first wife is built like an ox and all her babies were the size of sparrows. Too bad it couldn't have happened the other way around, much better for an ox to give birth to an ox and a sparrow to a sparrow."

Ophelia squinted with confusion and disgust. "Dear God, that's enough. I don't want to hear any more comparisons between your wives and the animal kingdom. How old was your second wife anyway?"

He looked up as if the ceiling held the answer, then pursed his lips. "She was fourteen. But she'd reached maturity."

Peter had retained his boyish good looks, although she calculated that he must be at least thirty. For many years, his companionship was all that had kept her from taking her life or turning to opium as so many other women did. His touch could melt her. And with him, she'd experienced such pleasure. She listened to him talk and realized he lacked basic intelligence. Had he been this stupid all along? Or was he drunk? Their relationship had been mostly one of passion. She'd been young then and seduced by his youthfulness and handsome features. Something deeper, and hopefully more substantial, characterized her relationship with Charlie.

She admonished him. "If you'd waited until the poor girl was grown before you married her and stuck a bun in her oven, she probably wouldn't have died. Have you ever thought of that? Maybe it's a sin to marry children."

Over his shoulder in the dining room, she saw that Charlie had noticed her long absence and was looking around the restaurant for her. She ducked down a little so he wouldn't see her talking to Peter. Because of her past, unfortunate encounters like this were bound to crop up in Ogden, which was just one more reason to sell the house and move.

Peter still blocked her way. Looking quite pathetic and remorseful, he reached up and spread his hands in the air, cupping them as if trying to catch an invisible bird. "She was so delicate. I just wanted to protect her." He closed his hands around the emptiness and they became fists.

"Then you should have left her alone. I'm sorry for her. But I'm not sorry for you. Please, step out of my way."

"Peach," he whispered, "can I still call on you?"

"Absolutely not."

"I'll pay," he pleaded.

Ophelia wanted to slap him. "If you ever come near me or my house, I will shoot you."

Charlie had spotted her. He stood and was making his way toward them from across the room. Peter followed Ophelia's gaze and saw him coming. He put his hands up and stepped back. "Okay, I'm going." He walked past her.

Charlie stood next to Ophelia and glared at Peter as he disappeared out the back door. With his hand at the small of her back, he guided her to their table, pulled the chair out for her, then sat down and straightened his tie.

Only one oyster remained, and her glass of ale was completely empty. She could have sworn she didn't drink it. She looked from the glass to Charlie.

"I didn't want your drink to get warm," Charlie explained. "So I drank it and ordered you another. You were gone so long, I thought maybe you drowned in that fancy water closet."

"Pardon my absence. A big pile of fresh bull-crap was blocking my path."

"Those Chinamen should have enough sense not to let a bull run loose in an oyster house."

"I suppose it's better than in a China shop," said Ophelia.

"Was he bothering you?"

Ophelia glanced toward the back of the restaurant and then back at Charlie. "I can handle myself, Charlie. But he's one of the many reasons I think it would be a good idea to sell the house and make a fresh start where no one knows me."

Charlie nodded. The waiter came, set two glasses of ale down, and asked if they would like anything else. They ordered roast duck and the waiter left them alone.

Through the window, they watched people and wagons pass. Ophelia couldn't stand it any longer. She leaned across the table. "What did Luther say? You didn't tell him about Ezekiel, did you? He knows about me. What if he knows where I live?"

Charlie gave her a reassuring look. "Don't worry, Ophelia. He expressed genuine concern for your welfare. And then he gave me the third degree—wants to make sure I'll be good to you. Honestly, I was expecting him to be hostile."

Unable to speak, Ophelia stared at Charlie in disbelief. She felt like someone had struck her in the stomach. Charlie squeezed lemon onto the last oyster and popped it into his mouth.

She managed to compose herself. "What about Ezekiel? Was there any mention of Ezekiel?" she whispered.

Charlie stared at the ruby necklace. "He's quite fixated on that necklace for some reason." He took a long swallow of ale.

"What about Ezekiel?"

"His name was never mentioned." He stared at the necklace.

"What is it, Charlie?"

He sucked air through his teeth and winced. "It might be a good idea to give it back."

Ophelia blinked and stared at him. "What? With everything you know about me and this necklace and what he did, I can't believe you'd even suggest that." Determined not to cry, she bit her lip and felt herself shake with anger and the pain of Charlie's betrayal.

Charlie shook his head. "I don't understand. A couple of months ago, you were desperate to rid yourself of that necklace. You threw it at my feet in Silver Reef."

"I wanted you to have it, not Luther. Don't you understand? I can never give this to him." She shook her head and sighed. "I should have left it for the ravens."

Amused, Charlie smiled and chuckled. "Rubies for the ravens!" He adopted a more serious tone. "Well, that probably would've been better than flaunting it. Luther became completely enraged as soon as he saw that necklace. I saw the anger flash in his eyes, even though he tried to hide it. Why don't you give the necklace to me? I'll give it to him, and then you'll be rid of him. That's all he wants."

The necklace felt heavy, like a shackle around her neck. Shame and anger filled her. Was Charlie on Luther's side? Did he think the whole thing was her fault? She wanted to know exactly what Luther had said to change his heart and mind. She tried not to show her hysteria. "I don't know what came over me this morning. You're right. I shouldn't have worn it. But I can't give it to him. That would be letting him win. What else did he say to you? It seems like you've changed your alliance from me to him."

"Ophelia, I was prepared to kill the man for you, remember? You wanted to make amends. I just acted cordial because we were paying a social call. I'm certainly not on his side. What on earth makes you think that?"

"You drank his spirits and said he was funny. Now you want me to give him the necklace."

"I'd drink the devil's liquor and probably laugh at his jokes, too. But that wouldn't mean I'm on his side. You can catch more flies with honey than vinegar."

"What exactly did he say while you were alone together, drinking in the study?"

Charlie sighed and took another long swallow of ale. He put his empty glass on the table, paused, and stared at it for a few seconds before answering. "The purpose of today's social call was so you could convince me the man has reformed and Ezekiel and I ought to give up our plans for revenge. Remember you said that you believe in redemption? Well, after our lengthy talk in the study, I concluded that besides the polygamous arrangement, which is fully sanctioned by the Mormons, and his strange obsession with that necklace, he has reformed and now expresses a genuine concern for your welfare."

Stunned and incredulous, Ophelia stared at Charlie. "A genuine concern for my welfare! Do you know what he did to me when you were in the garden picking peaches?" Ophelia sighed in frustration and took a long unladylike gulp of her ale. She tried to stay calm but couldn't keep the tremor from her voice. "He threatened to make my life a living hell. After he expressed such genuine concern to you, he grabbed me by the arm, right here." She pointed to the spot where Luther had grabbed and shook her. "And he threatened me."

Charlie furrowed his brow and looked concerned. "Well, I didn't know that. Why didn't you say anything? When did that happen?"

"As soon as you went outside with Widow Hopkins to pick peaches, he threatened me! Don't you see? He planned it. He's got everyone fooled—wrapped around his fingers. He's a charlatan, a confidence trickster, an imposter, and somehow he even fooled you, Charlie Sirringo, cowboy detective."

A look of hurt crossed Charlie's face, and Ophelia immediately wished her remark hadn't sounded so sarcastic. She softened her tone. "What did he tell you when you were alone? Please tell me."

"An entirely different story," said Charlie. "He said he never harmed you. He told me the Indians did it."

Sixteen

Something was broken between them. Charlie told her she'd been right all along, and they should drop the vendetta. Ophelia was sure his change of heart was because of what Luther had said in the study. She felt like she was a cracked egg, and her shell wasn't strong enough to hold her gooey insides. She moved with cautious fragility, as if any kind of impact would rip her open.

In Ogden, she felt like a sitting duck. Her instinct for flight grew stronger each day. Charlie was supportive of her plan to sell the parlor house and move to a new town. He didn't like running into men who had known her any more than she did. She didn't tell Charlie or Ezekiel that she had changed her mind about Luther—that she wanted him dead. Her thoughts often turned to him, and the various ways he might suffer and die. She both loathed and feared him. Every time she turned a corner, she expected him to be there. At night, his image and the feeling of his hands on her body haunted her.

Poor Nell was dying. With each passing day, her breath became fainter and her skin paler. Her daily struggle shifted from keeping dust and dirt at bay to the simple act of breathing. Ophelia was glad they'd decided to move her onto the porch where the breeze dissipated odors of death, and songbirds filled the pain-crammed spaces between her thundering coughing fits.

Nell didn't want a doctor or a priest. Ophelia sat for long

hours on a stool next to her cot. "Is there anyone I should inform?" she asked, already knowing the answer. Nell shook her head and closed her eyes. A list of undone chores grew, but Ophelia didn't want Nell to die alone. The time before death could be so quiet and still. There was much to learn in that time.

So stoic and silent was she, it was difficult to tell if Nell was in pain. She'd never been one to complain. Ophelia placed her hand on top of Nell's folded hands, patted them gently, and searched for something comforting to say.

"The very first day I arrived in Ogden, I met you there in the kitchen at Johnny's place. Pearl had all the working girls crammed upstairs. And there I was, scrawny and lousy, as naïve as a turnip. You gave me a big bowl of stew and an extra hunk of bread. All this time that I've known you, I never asked you about your past, your people, or anything."

Nell's eyes remained closed. Could she hear or understand? Was it worthwhile to stay and talk to her?

"I heard you were very beautiful once, and then something terrible happened."

Nell's eyes snapped opened; she shook her head and closed them again. Even before she fell ill, Nell hadn't spoken much, so Ophelia didn't expect much conversation. But she talked to her anyway, because she didn't want her to be afraid when she passed.

Ophelia began to tell her about her own life: how she'd traveled across the frontier by wagon train with the Mormons when she was little; how she'd carried her doll; how her mother had given her the ruby necklace; how Luther had tried to take it, and everything else that followed up until the day they'd met.

In telling everything to Nell, she realized that as a very young girl, she'd believed she was blessed until she fell from God's favor. But even in her lowest moments, some spirit was still inside her, giving her strength. And, by fortune or grace, the old Indian woman had found her and saved her life. Otherwise, she would've died alone in the desert at sixteen. It hadn't been her time. She believed it hadn't been her parents' time either. When they'd died she'd been terrified, grief-stricken, and lost.

But Nell was old; she'd been old since Ophelia had met her, and it was her time. Ophelia couldn't save her life. She could only help her pass. She smiled and whispered to Nell that after all these years, the ruby necklace was still hidden inside Dolly up on her bed. Nell's chest rose and fell with each breath, but her eyes remained closed, and Ophelia had no idea if she'd heard any of what she'd just said. She continued her story and told Nell all about her recent visit to see Luther and the trouble that had followed as a result.

At that, Nell's eyes snapped opened. She attempted to focus. Always a practical woman, the present interested her much more than the past.

She reached out and grabbed Ophelia's hand. Ophelia squeezed Nell's hand, reassuring her that she was still there.

Nell whispered hoarsely, "Never pick up broken glass with your bare hands."

Her hand grew so warm, it became hot. Ophelia pulled her hand away. She picked up Nell's wrist and turned her hand over. Tiny red spots of blood dotted her fingertips and palm. Ophelia lifted the burning hand into a ray of morning sunlight and inspected it. A tiny shard of glass glinted from a small cut on her palm. Other miniature bits of glass were coming out of her fingers.

She put down Nell's hand, wiped a bit of blood onto her apron, and tried to sound calm. "Nell, I'll be right back. I'm going to get some tweezers."

She rummaged around the house for the tweezers, found them in her sewing basket, and returned as quickly as she could.

Nell's eyes were closed and she was completely still—no breath or pulse. She'd slipped from life when Ophelia was gone. Maybe she'd wanted a private moment to die alone. Ophelia picked up her hand and stared—no signs of blood or glass.

She pulled the lightweight patchwork quilt up to Nell's chin and closed her eyes, wishing she could just leave her there because she looked so peaceful. With the extreme summer heat, they'd have to bury her quickly. And as soon as that was done, Ophelia would sell the house and leave town.

Ophelia hadn't told Ezekiel about the trip to Luther's house and didn't know if Charlie had told him anything about it either. She was afraid if she spoke to him, all of her anger, fear, and hatred toward Luther would come gushing out, and she'd end up agreeing to let him kill Luther. He returned from work early in the morning and, because of the heat, slept outdoors. He usually awoke by noon when the sun hit his face.

Ophelia stood over him with a cup of coffee. He stirred, blinked a few times, and put his forearm over his eyes to block the noonday sun. He sat up and rubbed his face. "I dreamt I smelled coffee."

"You weren't dreaming." She handed him the cup, smoothed her skirt, and sat on the grass next to his bedroll.

He took a sip and sighed with pleasure. "Thanks. What did I do to deserve this kind of service?"

"Nell just passed."

His face froze, and then he nodded in a resigned manner. "Sorry to hear it. I suppose we all knew it was coming. Were you close to her?"

"Yes, in a way, I suppose, as close as you can be to someone who hardly speaks. I met her the first day I arrived in Ogden. That was almost ten years ago. Zeke, something really strange happened. This morning glass started coming out of her hand—

tiny bits—for no reason at all. I went to get tweezers, and when I came back she was dead. I turned over her hand, but there was absolutely no sign of the glass or blood I'd seen. I swear; it was there." Ophelia searched her apron. "Look, look, see that red spot. That's blood from her hand—from the glass."

He looked at her, cocked his head, nodded, and took a sip of coffee. "Strange things often occur at the hour of death. It's unexplainable, so there's no sense in worrying about it or trying to figure it out."

"Well, when I came back, she looked very peaceful. It was probably the most peaceful death I've ever seen. I'd like to go that way."

He took another sip of his coffee and shook his head. "Not me. I want to go out fighting."

"Well, let's hope it doesn't happen any time soon for either of us. Nell was an old woman. She was ready. And I'm ready to sell the house now. Would you tell Belle London it's officially for sale? I'll consider her offer first." Ophelia stood and clasped her hands together. "Once we sell this place, there's no reason to stay here in Ogden. We could go anywhere, even Paris! Where do you want to go?"

He stared into his coffee, bit his bottom lip for a second, and then spoke in a serious tone. "Ophelia, I've got a job here now. Dora needs me."

"Dora? Who's Dora?"

"Belle London's real name is Dora: Dora Topham. Her maiden name was Hughes. She's married to a real bastard. He's more like a john than a husband."

"Have you met him?"

"No, he's been in Montana since early spring, but he's expected back any day now. I'm not looking forward to meeting him." Ezekiel stared past Ophelia at something in the distance.

"Do you always call Belle 'Dora'? Was that her idea?"

"Yes. She really trusts and depends on me, probably more than anyone else."

"Do you trust her?"

He shrugged his shoulders and changed the subject. "Charlie told me you went to see Luther and Widow Hopkins. What happened? You've seemed really nervous lately. Is it because of Luther? Is he the reason you want to move?"

Should she tell him that Luther was a danger to them both? Belle had him wrapped around her little finger. How could she warn him without sounding hypocritical? If she said anything against Belle, it would backfire. And yet, if he stayed behind in Ogden and Luther found him, the result could be disastrous. How could she convince him to move now that he was so enamored with Belle?

"Seeing Luther was—" She teetered on the truth; words that could incite him to kill the man. She decided against saying them. "Let's just say it was difficult. Later the same day, I had an unpleasant encounter at the Saddle Rock with a man I used to know. Do you understand how hard it is for me to live here? I'm trying to start a new life, but every time I go out, someone recognizes me. Nell's death is a sure sign that it's time to move. I can go somewhere no one knows me and live without daily disgrace. Won't you please come with me?"

"Ophelia, if anyone gives you trouble, all you have to do is tell Charlie or me. No one will hurt you with us around."

"You can't chase away this kind of trouble with fear and intimidation. You can't stop people from recognizing me and giving me dirty looks when I walk down the street."

"Who cares what they think? You'll never please those people. A lot of the people I've met here in Ogden admire you. They know you're the one who donated the money to keep the orphanage open. And you give those poor working girls at the cribs hope that someday they'll find something better."

Ophelia hadn't realized anyone knew about her donation. Her name certainly wasn't on the building or any donor list. She was grateful she'd never fallen low enough to have to become a crib girl, and although she felt bad for them, she didn't want to be their heroine. She wondered if Ezekiel's mixed race would always relegate him to the fringes of society. Would he be treated like a savage everywhere? Maybe in a big city or in Europe, people would think he was exotic and admire him.

She gazed at her brother. They'd been apart so long, and she was just feeling the bond between them again. "I'm glad you found some work here you like. But does that mean you want to stay? Here, in Ogden?" Her heart tightened. She'd assumed that they'd move away together. "If I sold the house, where would you live?"

"Please, Ophelia, you're my little sister, not my mother. I've been taking care of myself for a long time. You don't have to worry about me. Go—travel for a little while with Charlie. Take a trip to the ocean. You've always wanted to see it. As for me, I'll play it by ear for now. I just started working for Dora, and I'm not ready to leave yet. I won't stay forever. That's not my way. I lived in Silver Reef for three years. That was the longest I'd ever stayed put in one place."

He'd told her very little about his past, yet the scar on his cheek and all the others on his body had revealed that it'd been violent. He was lucky to be alive. "If I go, will you promise not to get too involved with Belle London? You have to be careful of women like that—"

"For God's sake, Ophelia! I wasn't born yesterday."

She put her hand up in a gesture of conciliatory regret. "Yes, okay, you're right. I apologize. Please tell her the house is for sale, and that I'd like to sell it as soon as possible." She stood and reached for Zeke's empty coffee cup. "I'm going to make arrangements for Nell. I'd like her to have a proper burial in a real cemetery. Lord knows, nothing else in her life was proper." She turned to leave and then turned back. "By the way, what did Charlie say happened when we visited Luther?"

"He just told me that you were right, and we should drop our revenge plan."

He'd hesitated so long before answering that Ophelia didn't quite believe him. "Is that all?"

He nodded. She left it at that, but all day while she was preparing Nell for burial, she wondered what kind of bullshit story about Indians Luther had told Charlie in the study that day.

Seventeen

Charlie helped Ophelia prepare the house for sale. They didn't speak about the necklace or their visit to Luther. He no longer appeared concerned about Luther. But Ophelia was worried Luther would figure out that she lived in Ogden and not California.

She and Charlie did speak about the future and where they'd go once the house sold. He talked about settling on a ranch in New Mexico, and she talked about boarding an ocean liner to Europe. They finally decided they'd travel, then settle somewhere, and that they'd start in Chicago, so Charlie could meet with publishers. He'd finally finished his autobiography. She'd also written her life story about how she'd gone from a Mormon girl to a madam, but she knew if she wanted to start a new life, it would be foolish to show it to anyone. Besides, people wanted to read about the exploits of cowboys and outlaws, not soiled doves.

Each day she woke up filled with dread, wondering if it was the day Luther would come for her. She had contemplated giving him the ruby necklace but couldn't bring herself to do it. She'd paid a great price for it, and although she could never have her virginity back, she could at least keep the necklace.

Ophelia was dressed in old clothes, pruning rose bushes by the front gate, when Mr. Topham and Belle appeared. They'd said they were coming the day after this one. She felt unprepared and somewhat irritated that they'd showed up a day early. But she couldn't imagine any respectable people who knew about the house's illicit past would want to buy it, so she acted as cordial as possible and tried to keep the desperation out of her voice.

Mr. Topham stood in front of Belle and blocked the gate. Impeccably dressed in a pinstriped suit and full of self-importance, he looked all around and tried to assess everything at once. He fixed his gaze on the house. Behind him and barely visible, Belle seemed small and meek. With the pruning shears still in her hand, Ophelia stepped out from around an overgrown shrub where she'd been secretly watching them.

"Hello," she called, and was about to introduce herself, but Mr. Topham interrupted her with a staccato voice that sounded like gunfire.

"We're looking for the lady of the house, Miss Peach Oatman."

Ophelia put down the sheers, took off her gardening gloves, and approached them with a smile. "I'm Ophelia Oatman."

"Oh, I thought you were a servant." He laughed, gave Ophelia a scrutinizing look, and raised his eyebrows. "Really, you're the famous Miss Peach? You look like a country bumpkin."

Belle grimaced and gave Ophelia an apologetic look.

"We were expecting you tomorrow," said Ophelia, trying to ignore his rude remark.

"Yes, I know. That's why I came today."

"Well, I don't suppose you're much interested in the roses, so let's go inside and I'll show you the house." She walked down the path and waved for them to follow.

Zeke was in the living room on a ladder, doing a last-minute repair on a crack in the wall.

"Ah-ha!" said Mr. Topham. "This is why I came today."

Ezekiel turned his head, gave the Tophams an obligatory cordial nod, and went back to his work.

Hands behind his back as if he were some kind of inspector, Mr. Topham strolled over and watched Zeke. "Fine work, boy," he said and turned toward Ophelia. "So, why should I buy this house?" He squeezed Belle's shoulder and shook her in a playful but rough manner, "Besides the fact that my wife here is nagging me to death."

Zeke had frozen, and Ophelia could tell he was trying not to lose his temper at being called "boy." Mr. Topham was at most a few years older than Zeke and treated him in a patronizing manner.

Ophelia imagined Zeke's former employer, Mr. Gee, had never called him "boy." But Mr. Gee was half-Chinese, so he probably understood Zeke's predicament. Zeke descended the ladder and put down his tool box. "I need something from the carriage house," he said and left the house. Ophelia noticed the strange way Belle watched him, but she tried to ignore it and focus on answering Mr. Topham's question.

"Why should you buy this house?" She repeated his question to buy time while she tried to come up with a good answer. "Well, the Doll House has been closed for over a year, and I still have men showing up. They're always disappointed to find out it's just a boarding house. As of now, no other establishment in Ogden has filled the place of the Doll House. After I show you the house, I'll show you the ledgers. They're a little confusing because Pearl used a code in case we were raided. But you'll see she made enormous profits."

"Was the house ever raided?" he asked.

"No. Pearl paid or gave favors to all the right people. All that information is included with the house." Her throat felt dry and hot from working outside and answering his questions. She covered her mouth and coughed. "Excuse me, I'm quite thirsty. Would you like some cold sangaree? It's homemade from the grapevine, and the iceman came this morning, so it's also cold."

She cleared her throat again. "I must wet my whistle or I'm afraid I won't be able to answer any more questions. I worked up quite a thirst out there, so I'm going to indulge. Will you join me?"

They accepted her offer. Belle sat on the parlor couch and sipped her drink. "Hits the spot, thank you," she said to Ophelia. She pointed to the chandelier. "Thomas, did you notice the chandelier?"

He'd downed his sangaree in one gulp and was inspecting the woodwork. "Hmm," he said and nodded. He still wore his hat, which was too tall and pompous for anywhere west of the Mississippi.

"Where are you from, Mr. Topham? Let me take your hat." Ophelia stood, brushed some dirt from her dress, and picked a leaf out of her hair. Next to Belle in a fashionable bustle and tight corset, she probably did look like a country bumpkin in her old housedress and garden boots. As common as she looked, she was comfortable and decided not to worry about her appearance. After all, the Tophams had come a day early.

He briefly turned his attention from inspecting the windowpanes and held out his hat for her to take. "As far as I know, I came from my mother, although the stork could've brought me."

Belle made an exasperated face and stood up. "Excuse me. I'm going to the privy and then to the garden for some air. I've seen the house, so please start the tour without me." She rushed out of the room.

Her husband barely noticed. He paced the room like a caged tiger, periodically stopping to hop up and down on the floorboards to check their strength. "I have cribs in Ogden, Cripple Creek, and Helena. They generate a handsome income. The structures are inconsequential—clapboard shacks that cost nothing and are worth nothing. But with the railroad junction here in Ogden, it's not just another boom and bust mining town, so I could justify the expense of a nice place. Dora wants to own and operate her own parlor house. She was always envious when she heard stories about you, and—what was her name?"

"Pearl."

"The fact that we heard of this house all the way in Cripple Creek impresses me. I'd like to see those ledgers. I'm still not convinced a parlor house generates more income than cribs. You can put rouge on a pig, but it's still a pig. Dress it up, call it by another name, but whoring is still whoring, don't you agree?"

Pearl would have known how to deal with this man. By now she would've sold him the house and God knows what else. "Actually, no, I don't agree. Cribs attract a much different type of man than a parlor house. If Belle can maintain a discreet parlor house establishment and attract the right customers, she'll be hobnobbing with some very rich and powerful men. In fact, Pearl had dirt on the entire town, and that became a kind of currency in itself. The difference between a crib and a parlor house is like that between a soup kitchen and a fine restaurant. Sure, they're both catering to the same human need, but in a much different way. I redecorated so the place looks like a respectable boarding house now, but when it operated as a parlor house, it had such an erotic ambiance, men would be aroused as soon as they walked in the front door. It was hard to get them to leave. And they came for more than just sex.

"If you don't see a difference between the cribs and a parlor house, then you may not be capable of understanding the complexity of these particular gentlemen. But I'm sure Belle does. Anyway, it's a big mistake to have a john hanging around a parlor house. Security men, yes, but no johns."

Mr. Topham glared at Ophelia, and she realized she had insulted him. His eyes betrayed a violent and calculating nature.

If she had a choice, she wouldn't do business with him.

"Well, Miss Peach, I'm interested in the bottom line. And I don't mean a woman's bottom; I mean how much profit is made. So I will take a look at those ledgers after you show me the house."

"Please, call me Miss Oatman."

He walked over to her and stood too close. "I'd also like to see what's under that frock. It's hard to understand what all the fuss was about when you're wearing a grain sack."

"Well, Mr. Topham, if you wanted to see me in a pretty dress you should have stuck to the day we agreed upon. Come on now, let's start with the kitchen. That's where all good things begin."

"Oh, I disagree. I'd say all good things begin in the bedroom."

He inspected the kitchen with the same scrutiny with which he'd inspected everything else. The house tour would take forever at this rate. But she tried to be patient and endure him, because he and his wife really were her only prospective buyers.

"Belle's done an impressive job while you were away, wouldn't you say? Upstairs girls working right above an ice-cream parlor is remarkable. Of all people, she could restore this place to its former glory. But you must give her a long leash and step back. The types of men who frequent parlor houses don't want a john hanging around."

He gave her a cold, yet smoldering look, which made her uncomfortable.

"Even if you decide not to open a parlor house, this is prime real estate and a very well-built house."

"Does this icebox come with the house?" he asked and opened it.

Irritated, she stared as the cold drained from the open icebox but decided not to scold him for it the way she would anyone else. "Yes, that can be arranged. As you can see, the kitchen is well-equipped. Another wonderful feature of this house is the root cellar. It's completely sealed off with a heavy door, so perishables keep for weeks even in summer. Come downstairs. I'll show you." She opened the door to the basement and went down the dark stairs before him. "Watch your head," she called back.

"Ow," he said, "too late."

While he was on the steps recovering from thumping his head, she lit a lamp and opened the door to the root cellar just to have a quick peek. It was the one place she hadn't had time to tidy. She gasped and slammed the door as fast as she could.

"What is it?" he called.

"Spider, huge spider, and mice too." She tried to erase the image of Ezekiel's buttocks and Belle's legs. Having relations in the root cellar! How could they? Were they crazy?

Mr. Topham stood in front of her, clearly displeased with bumping his head and being barred from the root cellar.

Ophelia shook her head and blocked the door. "Can't show it to you now, too messy, and there's a huge spider that could be poisonous, lots of legs. Sorry. Let's go back upstairs."

He took a step toward her. "I just hit my head coming down those damn stairs. I want to see it."

"Come back tomorrow, after I have a chance to clean it."

"Don't be ridiculous. I'm not afraid of a spider and some mice."

"No, no, I can't possibly let you see it in that condition." She shook her head and stood her ground in front of the door.

He took another step toward her. She moved close to him and seductively patted his chest. "How about this. How about I show you the bedrooms, and maybe even let you take a look at what's under this sack I'm wearing. All good things begin in the bedroom, remember?"

"Now you're talking." He reached around and squeezed her behind.

They heard a cough and turned toward the stairs. Charlie stood there looking hurt and stunned. In all the commotion, they hadn't even heard him. From the look on his face, she knew he'd overheard her proposition to Mr. Topham. She was horrified at what he must think of her.

Charlie was still as a statue, but she could see him turning away inwardly, shrinking back—disgusted. She wanted to explain it was a misunderstanding, and that Zeke and Belle were having sex in the root cellar, and she had propositioned Mr. Topham to keep him from opening the door. But she couldn't say anything. She tried by making faces and winking at him, but that only made him look more confused. How could she tell him what was happening without speaking? She paused and stood there for a moment paralyzed with shame and fear.

Belle and Ezekiel were lovers. Of course. How had she not seen it? There'd been a change in Zeke, and it was due to more than just finding employment. She'd been too preoccupied with her own troubles to see anything clearly. But why were they in the root cellar? Couldn't they control themselves? Were they crazy? Mr. Topham would probably kill them both if he found them. And they knew she was showing him the house, and sooner or later they'd get down there.

She had to think of something to say to Charlie. The look on his face made her ache inside. He stood still and expressionless. What could she do to tell him what was going on without revealing the situation to Mr. Topham? Nothing. There was nothing she could do.

"Charlie, hello, this is Mr. Topham. Remember I told you that he and his wife, Belle, are interested in the house? Mr. Topham, this is Mr. Sirringo. He helped me find my brother after we'd been separated for nearly ten years. I don't know what I'd do without Mr. Sirringo." Ophelia looked at Charlie with pleading eyes, imploring him to understand what she could not speak.

The cold way Charlie stared at her made her feel ashamed and hollow. He finally spoke. "Yes, well, I will let you get on with showing Mr. Topham the house. I'm sure he's very curious about the bedrooms. In fact, I'll take my leave and give you some privacy." He tipped his hat to them, turned, and climbed the stairs.

Her heart ached as her insides collapsed. "Charlie," she called. But he was gone.

EIGHTEEN

Stalling for time, Ophelia ascended the stairs to the second-floor bedrooms at a snail's pace with Mr. Topham trailing behind her. She fought a strong desire to run after Charlie and explain what had happened. Instead, she told Mr. Topham about the construction of the banister, the history of the wallpaper, and a humorous anecdote that involved a man falling down the stairs. Mr. Topham listened until he became irritated and gave her a little push from behind.

"Keep moving. I'm most curious about the bedrooms, Miss Oakman."

"Oatman," said Ophelia.

"Oh, whatever, let's get on with it," he grumbled.

She spoke in a loud, annoying voice, hoping Belle would hear and intervene. When she reached the door of the bedroom the boarder had recently vacated, she lingered and tried to make more small talk. Mr. Topham shoved her into the room. Had she really expected selling her house to a vile crib-operating pimp would be cordial? He advanced toward her with a wolfish snarl.

Just in time, Belle appeared in the doorway, out of breath with her hair slightly mussed. "So sorry for my absence. I was feeling a little dizzy. Must be the heat."

Ophelia stared at her and tried to make a gesture for her to straighten her hair. "Mrs. Topham! Why, there you are. Sorry to hear that. You don't look well."

Mr. Topham spun around. The sight of his wife took the wind out of his sails. "Where have you been? You've been gone for so long, I thought you'd hit the whiskey again. Since you've already seen the house, why don't you go take it easy downstairs?"

Belle tucked a few loose strands of hair behind her ears. "I added a little boost to my sangaree. That and the heat made me woozy. I took the liberty of lying down in one of the spare rooms. I hope you don't mind, Miss Oatman."

Ophelia smiled. "Oh, no, by all means, make yourself at home. I hope it will be your house one day. And I'm certain if I visit you and feel unwell, you'll return my hospitality."

"Why, of course."

"We may send some men in to keep you company." Mr. Topham laughed, pleased at his joke. All pretense of civility on his part had disappeared.

"Thomas, please!" cried Belle. "I'm interested in buying this house. Don't insult the owner. Where are your manners?"

He grinned. "Since you've been gone, we've dropped the formality. Let's quit pretending either of you strumpets are ladies." He turned to Ophelia, winked, and turned back to Belle, who still stood in the doorway. "Why don't you go lie back down, and I'll come fetch you when the tour is over."

Behind Mr. Topham's back, Ophelia shook her head violently and glared at Belle with a wide-eyed "don't-you-dare" expression.

"I feel much better now. And I'd like to see the house again. It's a big investment—our first real house. What do you think so far, Thomas?"

"I like what I see. But I'd like to see more, much more." He narrowed his eyes and looked Ophelia up and down. His wife ignored him. "Tell me, Miss Oakman, do you also wear bloomers?"

"No, not presently, but as soon as my bicycle arrives, I intend to."

"Ha! Your bicycle? I'd very much like to see you ride one of those contraptions. Why, we could probably sell tickets!"

Belle smiled. "You two are like bickering siblings!"

Ophelia tried to maintain a cordial manner toward Belle, but inside she was seething with anger. She cursed the woman for endangering her brother and causing Charlie to think she was a whore. But her desperation to sell the house trumped her anger. At the moment they were the only interested buyers, and the very walls seemed to be closing in on her. She had to escape and leave Ogden before Luther found her. It was only a matter of time. He would come for the necklace. He would come for revenge.

She wanted the Tophams to leave so she could go after Charlie. She couldn't bear what he must think of her. She looked at a clock on the mantel and pointed to it. "Oh, dear me, is that the time? While this is sooo lovely"—she tilted her head and smiled with sarcasm at Thomas—"We really must finish the tour. I'm deeply sorry. But I have another engagement. If this couple doesn't make an offer, you're more than welcome to come back and look again. There aren't that many houses of this quality so close to the train depot, but you may get lucky and find another one. If you return, I'll show you the root cellar, Mr. Topham. But first I must kill all the unsightly creatures I found in it."

Belle looked stricken and pale. She nudged her husband in the ribs. "Thomas! Should we make an offer?" she muttered out the side of her mouth. He grabbed her arm above the elbow, squeezed, and whispered something into her ear. She glowered at him.

Ophelia gave Mr. Topham her lawyer's card. When he wasn't looking, Belle mouthed the words "thank you."

When they were finally out the door Ophelia screamed in anger. "Ezekiel!"

Nineteen

For the first time since they'd been reunited, Ophelia was angry with her brother. When they were young, he'd mostly been a good brother, keeping an eye on her and protecting her from danger. But he'd played the occasional prank and made her the butt of jokes, especially when there were other boys around. All the rage she'd felt as a taunted, helpless child flooded back to her, as if she'd been the victim of a cruel sibling prank. She screamed his name again. He didn't answer her call.

She followed the sound of hammering to the carriage house, where he was concentrating on repairing a wheel axle as if nothing out of the ordinary had happened. He didn't acknowledge her as she glared at him with her arms crossed and her hands bunched into fists.

He finally glanced up. "Oh, hey there, Ophelia. How did it go? Did the Tophams like the house?"

His nonchalant manner infuriated her. She felt like putting his head on the anvil and bashing it in with a hammer.

"Charlie's gone."

"Oh? Where'd he go?"

"He heard me proposition Mr. Topham."

He screwed up his face in distaste. "You propositioned Mr. Topham? Eww, why?"

"I was trying to stop him from walking into the root cellar while you and Belle were fucking!" The word got his attention. He froze. She'd never talked that way in front of him. It was crude. She tried not to speak in a crude manner, even though she knew just about every crude word that existed, at least the English ones. Her anger made her whole body tremble. "Damn you!" she cried in exasperation. Her frustrated tears refused to fall. She didn't want to be a damsel in distress. "I love him, Zeke."

He put down his hammer, took a step toward her, held her by the shoulders, and looked into her eyes, something he rarely did even though she was his sister. "And I love Dora," he said.

"Oh, sweet Jesus, Ezekiel, why her?"

He began to answer, but she cut him off.

"Please, let's not talk about it now. There's no time. Help me find Charlie and tell him what happened. Can you imagine what he thinks of me?" Her voice rose with panic. She had to move, to do something before she lost Charlie forever.

Zeke stared at her in silence.

"I'll check all the saloons and other establishments on the north side of Fifth Street. You look on the south side," she said.

He ran a hand through his hair, picked up his hat, put it on, and shook his head. "I don't recommend you going into the saloons alone."

She showed him the small revolver she'd hidden in the folds of her dress. "There's no other option. I have to find Charlie." She turned and was half out the door when he spoke.

"Ophelia?"

"What?"

"Do you really think he's worth it, if this is all it takes for him to abandon you? He's so full of himself, I don't think there's room for you."

She glared at him and had to let her rage subside before she could even form words. "Set aside your distaste for him and help me."

"Distaste barely begins to describe my feelings for him. If I have to listen to another one of his self-glorifying stories, I will vomit an intestine."

Ophelia put her hands on her hips. "Do you realize he's actually a hero?"

"A hero in his own mind," Zeke mumbled.

"I think you're jealous because of all he's accomplished. What have you done in this life that's been heroic? Find him and explain the situation." Ophelia shouted, "This is your fault, Ezekiel!" She marched out and slammed the door of the carriage house.

Ophelia at least had the presence of mind to grab a bonnet from the house before she ran to Fifth Street, still wearing her shapeless gardening dress. The sun was fierce and burnt her face as she walked west toward the row of seedy saloons near Union Station. In her frantic single-minded search for Charlie, she was nearly run over by a wagon as she crossed the street.

She threw open the door of the first saloon, and a triangular slice of bright sunlight illuminated the darkness. Men shielded their eyes and cast irritated scowls at the source of the blinding light. It was as if she'd just turned over a rock or lit up a cave full of bats. She shut the door quickly, so as not to disturb the patrons or draw attention to herself. There was only one type of woman who went into a saloon alone. The saloons were deemed the "sewers of vice" by the respectable people of Ogden. And after many years of not entering one, Ophelia remembered why.

She stood on tip-toes and searched the dark establishment for Charlie. Men packed the bar and the tables. Except for a few barmaids, Ophelia was the only female. She knew there was a gambling den in the basement of one of the saloons, but she was leery of inquiring about it. There was no way she'd be allowed down there, even if she found it. Despite her common folksy dress and straw bonnet, men in the saloon still stared at her.

A drunk grabbed her by the elbow. "Would you like a companion? You sure look like you need a companion. Lemme be your companion," he slurred.

She figured, with her dress and bonnet, she could pass for an immigrant farmer, so she tried her best at imitating a Swede. "I look fer me huzbend. Cow birthing. Not well. You help?"

The man put his hands up to show they were as empty as his head. "I don't know much about birthing cows, miss. But I can buy you a drink. That'll help. Get 'er a bottle."

"You help? Yes?" Ophelia looked at the man, smiled crazily, and nodded. "Yes. You help birth cow. Yes. You help." She smiled and continued nodding as if her head was loose.

The man backed away from her into the crowded saloon. "Oh, no, not me. I'm not your fellow."

After finding no sign of Charlie, she left that saloon and searched five others. At every unwanted advance, she whispered into the man's ear, "I have syphilis," a trick from her youth that was effective for making men disappear.

Exhausted and nauseated from the heat and repulsive odors of the saloons, Ophelia stood under the shade awning of London's Ice Cream Parlor and wiped the sweat from her brow with a handkerchief. She tried to devise a strategy for dealing with Belle. She couldn't show her anger because she didn't want to jeopardize the house sale, but it was Belle's fault that Charlie left, and she had a duty to find him and explain the situation.

Both irritated and exhausted, she climbed the narrow stairs to the rooms above the ice-cream parlor and the adjoining brothel, which was also accessed from a saloon next door. Not yet busy with evening customers and there being many hours since the last train had passed through town, the place was quiet. A few girls wearing lacy undergarments lounged on chaises, fanned themselves, talked, and laughed.

Belle, fully dressed, emerged from a back room and smiled. "Ophelia! Great news! We are making an offer. Thomas just went out to see your lawyer. Did you run into him on your way here?"

"No." Ophelia caught her breath, took her bonnet off, and wiped her brow again. "Thank God."

"It's a generous offer. However, we want all the furniture and any décor you might have left over from the parlor house days. I don't know where you're going, but you'll have to leave most everything behind." Belle clapped her hands under her chin. "Oh, I'm so excited. It wasn't easy to convince Thomas to do this. He—"

Ophelia grew impatient and interrupted her. "Stop! Mr. Sirringo is gone. He heard me proposition your husband. Obviously, he doesn't know I was just trying to prevent him from going into the root cellar and finding you with Ezekiel."

Belle looked around nervously, put her finger to her lip, and pulled Ophelia into a private room. "Keep your voice down," she said.

"If it's such a big secret, why did you copulate with my brother in the root cellar with your husband in the house?"

"I know. I'm sorry. I have this little peccadillo; it's hard to explain."

"Well, thanks to you and Ezekiel, I may have lost Mr. Sirringo. I want you to find him and explain."

"Ophelia, there are plenty of men around. Please don't tell me you wanted to marry that one. I sincerely caution you against marriage. What do you want to marry for? You'll never earn back your reputation. I'd do anything to get rid of my husband. He's—"

Ophelia's voice shook when she said, "Mr. Sirringo is a good man, and I love him. You know love doesn't come easily for women like us. I'm not just playing with him like you are with my brother. What truly disgusts me is that my brother actually loves you. He can't see that when you're bored of him and he's no longer useful, you'll toss him away like garbage."

Belle shook her head, flashed a self-satisfied smiled, and whispered to Ophelia in an ethereal voice as if she were recanting a spell, "I brought him back to life. He'd been drinking the days away with no purpose and nothing to live for. If he hadn't started working for me, who knows what other vices he might have acquired, or reacquired. He told me I saved him. Those are his words."

Ophelia glared at her with burning anger, but she said nothing because she had to sell the house.

Belle nodded. "You see, he told me all about his problem, and how his former employer had helped him. Well, I did the same thing. Look at him now, mostly sober, well-dressed and well-groomed. He's full of pride and dignity."

"Maybe that's true now. But what happens when you break his heart?"

A smile crossed Belle's lips and she shrugged. "As you know, hearts are amazingly resilient. Just when you think you'll never love anyone again, someone else comes along."

"You may be so fickle, but Ezekiel's never been in love. Anyway, I don't have time for this." Ophelia pulled out a photograph of Charlie from a Denver newspaper. "Here, take this. Show it to your people and have them go out and look for him. You owe it to me."

Belle took the photo without urgency. "Nice picture."

"In order to sell the house, I have to find Mr. Sirringo. Without him, I'll have to change my plans."

Belle looked up from the photo. "I see. Well, I better get to it then."

Twenty

Ophelia walked home without urgency. Her manic, fruitless search for Charlie had drained her. It was still hot, but at least the sun was at her back. She looked behind her to the northwest where the sun was slowly sinking.

Continuing to search for Charlie was useless. He could be anywhere, even back at the house. Her shadow stretched before her like a stranger. She avoided the busy main street and turned down a side street. Her shadow disappeared. The street was completely empty except for the figure of a man in the distance. She stopped and watched him walk toward her. It was Charlie, encumbered with a suitcase and his walking stick. He looked up, saw her, and halted. They began to walk tentatively toward each other. Seeing him carrying his suitcase made her ache inside. She had to explain the situation before she lost him forever.

She stood close to him but not too close. "Charlie—"

He looked past her and spoke. "I received a telegram from the Pinkerton office in Denver. Apparently, there's a substantial sum of money there with my name on it. I need to collect it before it's forfeited."

"Charlie, the only reason I propositioned Mr. Topham was to keep him from going into the root cellar and finding Ezekiel and Belle. I opened the door before he came down the stairs and saw them together. Don't you see? I was desperate to keep him from going in there and was trying to divert him upstairs.

The whole thing is a misunderstanding."

He furrowed his brow, looking confused and skeptical.

"Do you believe me?" she asked.

"Ezekiel and Belle were together?"

"Yes."

"With her husband right there?"

"Yes!"

"Hmm." He shook his head, pulled out his pocket watch, and glanced at it. "Sorry. I've got to catch the six forty-five train to Denver."

"Charlie, I'm telling the truth."

"That doesn't change the fact that I need to catch the train."

"So that's it. You're running away without even talking about it, without giving me the benefit of the doubt."

"I'm not running away. I have to be in Denver tomorrow, or they'll forfeit my payment. Don't you believe me?"

Hurt and offended, she stared at him and tried not to cry.

He patted his vest and searched his pockets. "Here. I'll show you the telegram if you don't believe me." He fished in his pocket but came up empty. "Damn. I must've left it at the house somewhere." He looked at his pocket watch again. "Ophelia, I really must go. I'll be back. It'll only take a week at the most." He picked up his suitcase, turned, and rushed down the street toward Union Station.

She watched him, hoping he'd at least turn his head and wave, or blow a kiss, or do something to let her know things were all right between them. But he didn't. Over the years, she'd seen the backs of many men leaving a bedroom without looking back to acknowledge her. As a lady of ultimate accessibility, what could she expect? Certainly not respect or romance.

Although what just happened was probably the end of their relationship, the seeds of distrust had been planted by Luther when he took Charlie into his study. Damn him and his lies.

Luther had convinced Charlie that she was a hysterical, sex-crazy woman who couldn't be trusted. The day's events had just confirmed as much. Charlie probably thought she was a depraved Jezebel who'd do anything to sell her house.

Filled with self-loathing, she was frozen in the place where Charlie had disappeared from her view. She wanted to collapse on the ground, but someone turned the corner and was approaching, and she didn't want any human contact. So she turned, began to walk, and tried to keep all her feelings locked inside until she reached her house. A dog barked incessantly, the steam engine whistle blew, and the stagnant air was filled with suffocating aromas of freshly baked bread, manure, and meat from the smokehouse.

She had found Charlie and lost him anyway. What could she have done to convince him she was telling the truth? Should she have begged, cried, and pleaded? If Belle or Ezekiel had found him first, it would've made a difference. Her sordid past cast a shadow of doubt over everything she did and said. Ever since the day he'd been alone in the study with Luther, she'd seen mistrust lurking in his eyes. Luther had poisoned Charlie against her with lies. Why else would he go from wanting to kill the man to suggesting she return the ruby necklace?

Ophelia should've known it would end like this. How could she be such a fool? And now what was she to do? Travel alone, unaccompanied? Maybe she would buy a first-class ticket and take the railroad all the way to the ocean, but which coast? She'd been so excited to travel with Charlie and then buy a place somewhere that Ezekiel would also like to settle. Everything was ruined now, thanks to Belle and Ezekiel.

Several times on her way home, she felt the will to go on drain from her. The sight of the house brought relief, until she realized it would soon be gone, and then her heart raced. She walked through the front gate, around to the backyard, and looked at the house as if it were somehow alive. The spot where Charlie had unrolled his bedroll and slept in the grass was still matted. She fell to the earth, pulled the grass between her fingers, and let all her tears and anger release until the air grew cool and she felt something wet on her cheek.

"Miss Havisham, I thought you were dead," she said to Nell's old cat that'd been missing since the day Nell was buried.

The cat nudged her and purred in circles around her head until Ophelia roused herself and stood. She picked up the cat, feeling mostly bones and fur. "Let's get you some food," she said. The back door was unlocked. She cradled Miss Havisham, walked into the house, then set her down and locked the door behind her. The house was completely empty, so she placed her little revolver on the kitchen table, and peeled off the dirty, sweat-stained gardening dress she'd been wearing since morning.

What a terrible day. How quickly everything had turned to shit. She opened the icebox and poured the cat a bowl of milk and herself a glass of sangaree. While the cat lapped the milk, she gulped the sangaree, then filled her glass again.

With the glass in her hand, she wandered into the parlor, feeling like a ghost, with so many memories and an uncertain future. She sat at the piano, which she'd have to leave there along with almost everything else. Earlier, in preparation for showing the house, she'd set a vase of flowers on the piano. She set her drink down next to them, not putting anything under it, not caring if the wood stained. Love had escaped her, but at least she still had money.

She played "Hard Times Come Again No More," the song she and Charlie had heard in Frisco, the song everyone knew about being poor and destitute. Charlie had been touched by the song, and she recalled feeling so much affection for him because of it. In an attempt to cheer up, forget about Charlie, and stop wallowing in self-pity, she reminded herself that for once in her life she wasn't destitute and poor. Life could be far worse. So many opportunities were available now that she was wealthy.

Wealthy people could do things on their own. They didn't need love or approval. Pearl had taken care of her, and she'd never gone hungry or without nice clothes. But Pearl had controlled everything. Ophelia had seen her as a parental figure, yet now that she had a grasp of the finances, it often angered her that Pearl had waited so long to release her from her duties as a parlor house girl. Keeping her hadn't been financially necessary as Pearl had claimed.

Her bare buttocks were sticking to the piano bench, and there was a possibility Ezekiel would return, so she took her drink and climbed the stairs to her room to find clothes. She thought about a bath, but the sangaree and all her crying had made her too tired to bother drawing one. Ophelia had never fully appreciated how much around the house Nell had taken care of until she got sick and died.

She put her drink on the bedside table, flopped down on her bed next to Dolly, and closed her eyes. Her head spun with thoughts, emotions, and sangaree. Her eyes snapped open and she looked at Dolly.

What if Charlie had stolen the necklace? The sound of her panicked breathing filled the room. He knew where the necklace was hidden. But why would he steal something she had offered to give him? Maybe Luther had convinced him to get it for him. What would she do if Dolly was empty? The betrayal would be more than she could bear. And could she live without the necklace? It had some kind of hold on her. Maybe it would be for the best if it was gone, but not this way.

In an agonizing moment of uncertainty, she hesitated, closed her eyes, and braced for the worst. She turned over Dolly, put her fingers inside the slit in her back, felt the necklace, and pulled out the strand of precious rubies. She lay on her back and sighed. Her heart thumped fast and loud, yet relief washed over her.

Of course, Charlie wouldn't steal her necklace. He was a teller of tall tales, but a man of honor. She should be ashamed to think such things of him after all he'd done. She opened her eyes and stared at the necklace, mesmerized by its old-world beauty, and whatever else it was that cast such a strange spell over her.

The memory of Luther's face came to her, his murderous eyes when he'd seen her wearing it. He would find her and come for the necklace. There was no question in her mind. She was surprised he hadn't found her already.

The safe in the study was a much more secure place to keep the necklace, but the rubies seemed to belong inside Dolly. Who would think a worn, ratty doll contained something so priceless? Ophelia got up, smoothed the blankets, put the necklace back, and placed Dolly amongst the pillows. She dressed in a light nightgown, grabbed her glass, and went down to the second floor.

Charlie had taken everything from his room. Even the bureau drawers were empty. She noticed two pieces of paper on the floor under the bed. She had to lie on her stomach on the dusty floor and extend her arm to reach them.

The telegram! He hadn't been lying. She held it to her heart and, for the first time, felt a glimmer of hope that he might return. The other paper was a tattered photo of a little girl. Ophelia stared at it and squinted. She had the same olive skin tone and brown eyes as Charlie.

The house was so quiet, she began talking aloud to herself. In the kitchen she retrieved the revolver from the table. On second thought, she put the revolver back down, and fetched Nell's old shotgun out of the pantry. Even though it was still warm and she was enjoying the breeze from the opened windows, she shut and locked every one. The house grew even quieter, and with the windows closed, she couldn't hear the birds or crickets, only the deafening tick-tock of the hall clock. She filled up her glass again and, with the shotgun, sat on the front porch like a sentry keeping an eye out for intruders.

The hedges were tall enough that no one could see her from the street. The last thing she had said to Zeke was cruel, and she felt guilty. She wanted him to come home so she could apologize. He was, after all, a man. She couldn't really blame him for succumbing to Belle. She couldn't imagine why they'd risk an intimate encounter when her husband was so close—some kind of thrill-seeking perversion on Belle's part, she supposed. She hoped it wasn't something they did all the time, because sooner or later they'd get caught.

If she could convince Zeke to leave town with her, she might be able to save him. She cast anxious glances toward the street and imagined Luther coming in through the gate. She'd aim the gun at his heart and put a bullet in him. She'd kill him, just like that, no discussion, and no time for lies. Finally she rested the gun across her lap, listened to the trees and shrubs rustle, and watched the sky grow blue and purple.

The front gate creaked. She lifted the gun, but lowered it when she saw Ezekiel, relieved that he'd returned. She realized she was probably being unduly suspicious and should go to bed. He approached cautiously with an uncertain look on his face.

"Sorry. This is not meant for you," she said, indicating the gun.

He walked up the stairs, handed her a bouquet of flowers, leaned on the post, and crossed his arms. "I know you're mad, but I hope not mad enough to shoot me."

Ophelia smelled the flowers and smiled. She put them in her

empty glass and placed it on the table beside the chair. The glass began to topple over, but Zeke reached out and caught it before it fell and shattered.

"Well done," she said.

He placed the glass of flowers on the porch floor. "Ophelia, are you all right? What happened? Did someone threaten you?"

She sighed, stood up, stretched, put her hands on her hips, and gazed out into the dark. Her head spun a little. She leaned on the porch railing and steadied herself. She looked back at Zeke and the big house that would soon not be hers. "I'm all alone. Charlie's gone. He took a train back to Denver. I don't know if he's coming back."

Zeke sighed, bit his lip, shook his head, and closed his eyes. "I'm so sorry. I wish I could've told him what happened and straightened this mess out. Listen, Ophelia, you're not alone. I'm here now." In an unusual gesture, he put his arms out to embrace her.

She grabbed him around the waist and squeezed as if she were wrapping herself around a tree, a tree she grew up with that was in danger of being cut down. She didn't let go. Finally, he stepped back a little and looked down at her. With his rough thumbs, he wiped tears from her cheek. "I'm not working tonight. I'll be here with you. What are you afraid of all of a sudden? Is it because Sirringo's not here? Do you think someone wants to hurt you or rob the house?"

She hadn't told him about Luther's threats. She didn't want any trouble for him. And with Charlie constantly at her side, she'd felt as though Luther couldn't get to her. Charlie wasn't a large, fearsome man like Ezekiel, but he had a reputation as a crack shot, and he never strayed too far from his precious pearl-handled Colt. She didn't answer.

"Are you afraid of drifters, a former customer, that whiskey guy?"

"How do you know about him?" she asked.

"I hear enough gossip at the brothel to fill the ocean."

Ophelia smiled. "How about a drink and some dinner?"

"I appreciate the offer, but I have the feeling you're dodging my question. Who are you afraid of? Why are you sitting here with a gun and the house all locked?"

"How come you're not working?" she asked.

"Okay, let's go inside and I'll tell you all about it. I'm parched. This heat is really something for mid-September. It feels like Grafton."

They went into the kitchen. He took off his jacket, unbuttoned his shirt, and rolled his sleeves. "Good God, Ophelia, it's too hot in here." He opened the kitchen windows.

She took out ham and cheese from the icebox.

"Dora gave me the night off. She feels bad about what happened today. And tomorrow night, I'll have to be there the whole night. Topham has to go back to Montana. He confided in me that he suspects Dora has a lover and told me to keep an eye on her." He laughed to himself and shook his head. "Of course, he has no idea it's me. Nobody does."

Ophelia placed the food and nearly empty pitcher of sangaree on the table. "I wouldn't have guessed it either, until I saw you together today." She shook her head and made a face at him. He blushed. "Now that I look back, it all makes sense," she said.

"So why wouldn't you have guessed we're a couple? Because she's young and pretty, and I'm a scar-faced half-breed? I suppose you don't know what she sees in me."

Ophelia shook her head. "That's not true. You're a strong and handsome man, even with the scar." She pointed at him. "Put that scar on my face, and it would be a different story." She took bread out of the breadbox and put two plates on the table, deciding it would do her good to eat as well.

They ate and talked. The food tasted good. She wanted to make amends with her brother. "I'm sorry for the things I said to you. What man could resist Belle? And I forgive you for not using good judgment and having a tryst in the root cellar with her. It was her idea, wasn't it?"

"Of course, it was her idea. Would I ever suggest something so coarse? You know she regrets the marriage and was earning more money on her own. But she felt like she needed a man's protection. Too bad she didn't meet me first."

Ophelia stared at him, shocked at how hard he'd fallen for Belle. "Well, she didn't. And I would put an end to the affair. Sooner or later, Topham will find out, and then he'll kill you. I'm sure he'd sell her to the highest bidder, but only on his terms."

"You never know. He may have some kind of accident first and cease to be a problem."

Ophelia put down her ham sandwich. She could barely chew the food still in her mouth.

"Ezekiel, no. Put that thought right out of your mind!"

He cocked his head sideways and grinned at her. "Have you lost your sense of humor?"

"I'm afraid it got on a train to Denver."

"Do you want me to go to Denver and set things straight?"

"He said he's coming back."

"Do you believe him?"

"I didn't at first. But I found this telegram under his bed." She took the telegram out of the book she'd been trying to read and handed it to him. "I also found this." She handed him the picture of the little girl.

Ezekiel looked at them both then focused on the girl and cocked a brow. "Hmm, she looks like him."

Ophelia cleared the plates and food. "I'm going to bed," she said.

"Listen, in case I don't see you in the morning . . . are you going to be all right here alone tomorrow night?"

"Of course," she said and smiled. "I've got Nell's old shotgun. And I won't be alone, because Miss Havisham has returned. What could possibly happen?"

"Forget about that old gun. I'm going to leave you my Winchester."

Twenty-One

Luther tried to calm the thumping in his chest as he carefully opened the gate. On the tidy path to the front porch, the crickets and cicadas chirped. The house was tucked away on a quiet street away from the town hub. It didn't look like the sort of place that had once been a brothel.

So much work had gone into finding Ophelia and making sure she'd be alone. Obsessive thoughts about the necklace had plagued him ever since she'd strutted into his living room with it around her neck. All these years he hadn't known for sure if she had it, but his hunch was she had, and now he was vindicated.

The front door's decorative beveled-glass window distorted his view into the house, but it appeared no one was home, so he retrieved the key nippers and jimmy from his coat pocket and wiggled them into the lock. The door clicked open. He walked in, looked around, and shut the door as slowly as he could, although it creaked anyway. Was there a dog? He hadn't planned for a dog. No, it would've barked by now. He sighed in relief; he'd always rather liked dogs and wasn't prepared to kill one.

In the hallway, a clock ticked loudly, but otherwise the house was absolutely still, giving him the impression it was empty. The two men were definitely gone. He'd heard there'd been an old hag who'd recently passed, so he'd expected Ophelia to be there alone. But there was no sign of her. Still, he was cautious as he rummaged through drawers and cabinets, searching for the necklace.

As his search turned up nothing, he grew louder as anger and impatience overtook his caution. In the study, he found a safe hidden in a closet. The necklace could be there. As stubborn as Ophelia was, he'd have to torture her to get it open.

The second floor was mostly empty bedrooms and a door leading to the attic. He opened the door and immediately smelled woman—traces of perfume and that other vague odor women had. The stairs creaked under his feet, and perspiration trickled down his temple as he leaned on the banister and climbed toward the faint light under the door at the top of the stairs. Maybe she'd heard him come in and was cowering in a cobweb-filled corner. As he ascended, the air grew warmer and warmer until he reached the top of the stairs, pushed opened the door, and felt a cooling breeze from an opened window.

He assessed the room. The bed and other furniture revealed it was a bedroom. Unlike the bedrooms on the second floor, this one was currently in use. A white wicker rocking chair sat in the corner. Drenched with sweat, Luther peeled off his jacket, realizing too late he should've taken it off before he lumbered up the stairs. He draped the jacket over the chair, ran a hand through his damp hair, and sat. The chair groaned under his weight. He sighed and wiped his brow with a handkerchief.

White walls, white lace curtains, and white wicker furniture—the room looked more like a virgin's sanctuary than a whore's chamber. In the middle of the bed, a decrepit doll sat on a patchwork quilt. Propped by ruffled white pillows, she stared at him from her one black eye with the menacing presence of an eye-patched pirate. He stared back at her for a moment, was filled with a vague sense of recognition, and then remembered it was Ophelia's doll. He could picture it on her rickety cot in Grafton.

A flutter turned his gaze to the open window, where the breeze stirred the curtains—white curtains—so much white for a whore's bedroom. Disappointed to find the house empty, he stared at the billowing curtain and wondered where Ophelia could be. She was bound to return soon. He figured he should go back downstairs, so he could grab her before she noticed there'd been an intruder. A nice-looking Winchester was propped against the wall behind the curtain. With effort, he unwedged his large frame from the small wicker chair, went over, and picked up the gun. He sat back down with it in his lap and inspected it.

He looked up from the Winchester, surprised to see a bare leg pop through the opened window. Ophelia, with a bottle in one hand and a glass in the other, didn't notice him. She'd been drinking on the roof and teetered a little as both feet touched the floor. She stood with the bottle and glass, wearing only a white slip. He shook his head in disapproval—so much white. She saw him, dropped the glass, and screamed. When she stopped screaming, he smirked.

"Better be careful," he said. "You don't want to cut yer foot there." He pointed at a large shard of jagged glass.

She stared at the gun.

He stood, placed the Winchester in the corner behind the chair, and walked toward her. "Don't worry. I'm not going to shoot you." Her expression made him want to torture her slowly. He smirked again. "My plan was to wring your scrawny neck."

She was breathing fast—panting like a trapped animal. He had her cornered. Unless she jumped out the window, there was no escape. He grasped her neck in a possessive, yet seductive, manner. She struggled. He squeezed until she couldn't move. Before he knew what had happened, his crotch burned with ferocious pain, and he realized she'd kneed him in the groin.

He let go of her and doubled over, holding himself. "Bitch!"

he yelled. She made a sudden quick move toward the door. He grabbed her arm and yanked her back. She struggled and writhed and flopped around like a hooked fish. The pain in his balls, her defiant look, and the chaotic slippery movement of her limbs infuriated him, and he struck her as hard as he could across the face.

She fell to floor from the force of his blow. Stunned and quiet, she sat there, crumpled, with her head down, and her hand pressed to the spot where he'd struck her. She didn't weep or whimper or beg him for mercy. Such pride. Just like her mother.

"Too proud to cry? Remember, pride before destruction and a haughty spirit before the fall," he said.

His sister had been so full of rebellious convictions that they had destroyed their family. Ophelia looked like her mother. All the hatred and bitterness he harbored against his sister were directed at her now because she was alive and rebellious, had tried to kill him, and had stolen the necklace. Somehow, he'd have to make her tell him where it was before he killed her.

"Were you planning to shoot someone with that gun? Maybe you were going to shoot yourself, because you're all alone. Too late. I'm here. And I will kill you slowly and painfully if you don't give me that necklace. You should've jumped off the roof. It would've been much more pleasant than facing my wrath." He reached down and stroked her hair. "Although, if you beg hard enough, and give me the necklace without a fuss, I might let you live."

Her lack of response infuriated him. He grabbed her hair and pulled her to her feet. With her hair as a cord, he yanked her head back. She closed her eyes and winced, but still refused to utter a sound, or even look at him.

"Where is the necklace?" he demanded through gritted teeth. She didn't answer or open her eyes. He let go of her hair and squeezed her throat.

She went from white to blue and finally opened her eyes. Relieved to see in them the terror he craved, he eased his grip, but kept his hands around her neck. She gulped air and hyperventilated.

"Now where is the necklace? Is it in the safe downstairs?" he whispered.

She didn't answer. He squeezed her throat again. Her eyes bulged. She lifted her hand. He eased his grip. Between gasps she pointed to the bed, to the pillow, where the wretched doll was propped. He let go of her neck, pushed her to the ground, picked up the pillow, and tore it to shreds. No necklace. White feathers floated around the room, lifted by the breeze and illuminated by moonbeams filtering in from the open window.

Surrounded by glowing white feathers, he approached Ophelia, who was doubled over, gasping for air. He was about to assault her again. She shook her head and pointed at the one-eyed doll, which had been tossed when he grabbed the pillow and now lay at the end of the bed next to him. He picked up the doll, found the gash on her back, slid his fingers inside, and split her in two. As he grasped the chain of beautiful red rubies, his fingers trembled. He fell to his knees, held the rubies to his lips, kissed them, and wept.

"Mother! Mother!" he cried and trembled. Luminous white feathers floated all around him. "Why did you forsake me?"

Twenty-Two

Ophelia hyperventilated and then slipped into another realm—perhaps death. She'd never know for sure. Upon her return, she found herself in her attic bedroom, with Ezekiel standing over her; a halo of white feathers had caught in his hair and waved like tiny filaments. She thought she was in heaven until she noticed the grotesque body of her uncle—breathing but unconscious, lying on the floor, blood dripping from a cut on his head where Ezekiel must've struck him.

Something indescribable had happened while she was unconscious. Had it been death or some sort of a transition between life and death? Whatever it was, she'd never forget nor deny it. There'd been no man on a throne in the sky. She was thankful for that, because a man had just strangled her, and the last thing she wanted was to see another one. She'd returned to this world from another one where form had hardly any substance and changed rapidly. What she'd seen was beyond words, and she knew instinctively not to try and explain it to anyone.

Or, could it be brain damage? Had the strangulation caused brain damage? Was her experience an elaborate hallucination? She stared at the feathers still floating around the room and looked at her brother, the angel, Ezekiel.

He crouched beside her. "I was going to shoot him. But I didn't think it was a good idea, considering the mess it would've made and the house sale and all." He looked at Luther, shook his head, and scrunched his face in distaste. "Also, he was lying there on the ground, crying like a baby for his mother."

Luther groaned, writhed, and lay still. Ophelia and Ezekiel stared at him with revulsion and wonder.

Ezekiel shook his head. "To be honest, it didn't feel right to shoot a man who was crying for his mother." He inspected her neck and swollen cheek. "Don't worry, you won't ever have to look at him again. I'll take care of him."

Ophelia peered at the large body of the man who'd tried to strangle her. She tried to take a few deep breaths; doing so made her lungs and throat burn. A large spider dangled from a web in the corner of the room and was working to repair her home, which had been damaged in the feather storm. "No. Don't kill him. We can no more kill Luther than that dear spider."

Ezekiel looked at the spider and back at her with concern. "I can kill both him and that spider, no problem."

"No more killing. You've got to understand, when I was passed out, I saw all the killing and where it leads." In a daze, she stared after the memory. "After they kill you so many times, you're free. The veil lifts. Fear of death is gone. You see, we'll all walk through death's door someday. It's not when that matters, it's how. When we go, we must go in peace and bear no man a grudge, even our worst enemy."

She sighed and squinted at Luther. "Before he came, I was sitting on the roof, consumed with self-pity and a little drunk. I wanted to die. I almost jumped off the roof except, as mad as I was, I wouldn't do that. And with my luck, I'd just break my back and not die."

"Ophelia, I'm sorry about the misunderstanding with Siringo. I'll find him and make it right. I promise."

She shook her head, stared at Luther, and nodded at his body. "Right now, we have more pressing concerns. Take that big baby downstairs and tie him to a kitchen chair." A breeze chilled her shoulders and she hugged herself. "I'll put some clothes on and be right down."

Ezekiel shook his head and sighed. "He's a beast, not a baby, Ophelia. It'd be best if I took him outside and put a bullet in him—end his suffering and ours."

"Maybe inside every beast is a baby."

"He almost killed you."

"But he didn't. Here I am. Killing is over for me. I saw awful things, Zeke. I saw so much killing. I saw the whole world at war. And I saw how it ends if we continue on this way. I can't change the world, but I can change myself. Anyway, I don't want to be haunted by him the same way Red Farrell haunts me."

Barely conscious, Luther still clutched the necklace in his hand. Ezekiel pried it from his fingers and pressed it into hers.

She held it and rolled a ruby between her thumb and index finger. "We need to uncover our family secrets and find out why he's so obsessed with this necklace."

Ezekiel dragged Luther out of the room by his legs. The steady rhythm of his head hitting each step as they descended the stairs made Ophelia cringe.

"Try not to turn his brain to mush, we need him to answer some questions," she called over the thumping.

Twenty-Three

Barefoot, Ophelia remembered the broken glass and bent down to pick up a shard so she wouldn't cut her foot on it. Nell's dying words came back. "Don't pick up glass with bare hands." She shook her head at the strange appropriateness of Nell's words, then tiptoed to the closet. The worn leather of Red Farrell's boots yielded to her touch. She had meant to get rid of them so many times, yet they sat there on a hatbox in the crawl space next to her armoire. If she let Ezekiel kill Luther, she could be cursed with his ghost too. Was Red Farrell's ghost real, or was it a manifestation of her guilty conscience? He felt both real and unreal.

She stared at the boots and heard his voice. "You're the one holding on to me. You know that, don't you?" he said.

She looked behind her at the empty bedroom, pulled the boots on, sighed, and slipped on a dressing gown. Even though he didn't have a physical form, she could feel Red's presence. Had he been there when Luther was strangling her? Probably not; he most often showed up when she was dressing or bathing. She grabbed a broom and swept the glass into a pile, then sat on the bed and pulled off the boots. She was tempted to toss them out the window. Instead, she placed them on the sill.

"I bare you no grudge for shooting me," said Red. "If I'd been in your place, I would've fired too. I've forgiven you, but you haven't forgiven yourself."

She felt warm breath on the crook of her neck.

"Now, how about a kiss?"

Ophelia shuddered and brushed a shiver away. Red was a frisky pest. She stood, put her hands on her hips, and glared at the boots. "Go away," she said.

"If that's what you want, release me. I was a bad man. But being killed by a young girl was a more shameful death than I deserved. Hell, I survived some of the bloodiest battles of the war, and then I got done in by you." He chuckled.

Ophelia grinned. "At least you can laugh about it."

"Better to laugh than cry. There's no quality I despise more in a man than self-pity." Ophelia took the boots from the windowsill and climbed through the window. She stood on the roof in the moonlight and looked down at them. "What should I do about Luther?"

Red laughed almost as hard as he did on the day she killed him. When he finally collected himself, he said, "That's up to you, missy."

She sighed, smiled, wound up like a baseball pitcher, and threw the left boot as far as she could. Losing her balance a little, she stumbled and nearly slipped off the edge of the roof. She stepped back to a safer spot and threw the right boot like a disk, hoping to gain a little more distance without falling. "Goodbye, Red," she called.

As she was climbing back through the window, a howl rang through the night, sounding like a wolf or an infant or some combination of both. A few seconds later the pack's chorus answered the lone cry. Red Farrell was finally home.

Twenty-Four

Ophelia looked around the room and jumped when she saw the wicker chair. Luther's jacket was draped over it, and for a second she had thought it was him—another object taking on humanness.

A strange quality imbued the world. The very air around her seemed to buzz and vibrate. Was her mind gone? Her brain damaged? The feathers had fallen to the floor, but they stirred when she walked through the room, creating an ethereal swirl about her feet. She summoned her courage and lifted the coat. From a pocket, she retrieved a worn, dog-eared book. She held it in her trembling hand, then carried it and the coat downstairs to the kitchen.

Ezekiel had bound Luther to a chair at the table.

As he came back to consciousness, Luther's head bobbed, and he drooled and muttered to himself.

Ezekiel placed a bottle and two glasses on the table. Ophelia went to the cabinet, got another glass, and placed it on the table in front of Luther. She took a pitcher of cool lemon water from the icebox, poured herself some, and offered some to Ezekiel.

He shook his head. "I need something stronger than that."

She downed the lemon water. Her brain practically exploded with the cool lemony sensation. She poured a glass of liquor each for Ezekiel and Luther, and slid Luther's glass toward him, just out of reach.

Ezekiel watched her with narrowed eyes and a disgusted

expression. "What are you doing? I wouldn't even let that man drink my piss."

"The smell might rouse him out of his stupor."

"Why do you want to rouse him? So he's awake when I kill him?"

She shook her head and placed the book from Luther's pocket on the table but didn't open it.

"Ophelia, I need to tell you something."

She waited, but Ezekiel didn't speak. "Well, tell me something," she said.

"Luther paid Belle to keep me at her place, so he could come here and do this. She took his money. But she didn't go through with it. As soon as she told me, I came. She's a decent woman." He shook his head and blew air through his mouth. "Good God, though, I'm glad she didn't wait any longer. I got here in the nick of time." He winced as he inspected the injuries to his sister's face and neck, and then glared at Luther.

Ophelia stared at the hardened man who'd gone soft with puppy love for a whore. "I wonder how he found out about you, and how he knew you worked for Belle. I guess he didn't realize how much she likes you." She smiled. He stared at his drink and blushed. "You know," said Ophelia, "I think he also arranged the telegram to Charlie. Maybe it wasn't just an excuse to leave me because of what happened." She got up and went to a kitchen drawer where she'd put the telegram and photo.

Twenty-Five

The sweet, fiery vapors of liquor brought Luther back to his senses. He blinked and tried to focus, which caused an excruciating pain in his head. The ironlike smell of blood and a sticky sensation on his scalp must've been where the Injun had struck him. He instinctively reached up to touch the wound, but his hands were bound. Among all his other aches and pains, he felt the spiny rope digging into his wrists. Objects on the table in front of him became clearer as he regained his focus: a shot of liquor that smelled like brandy, his key jimmy, pistol, and knife. Across the table, Ophelia and the Injun kid were busy inspecting his other things.

The Injun kid wasn't a kid anymore. He was a tall, muscular, formidable man. Luther figured even if he hadn't snuck up and conked him on the head, it would've been a struggle to fight him. Noticing he was conscious, Ophelia and Zeke looked up and stared at him. He wracked his brain for a scheme, a story, something he could say or do that might save his life.

He focused his efforts on Ezekiel. "Haven't seen you since our card games. Remember those? What did we play for—pecans?"

"Walnuts," said Ezekiel in such a cold-blooded, matter-of-fact way, it gave Luther a little chill.

"You know, I never did get to apologize for telling the Mormons about your dealings with Black Hawk. Why, the Indians, they're your people, and you certainly have a right to fraternize. But you do understand that I had a duty."

Ophelia looked like she'd seen a ghost and turned a shocked and confused look at her brother. He didn't look at her. He kept his "I'll slit-your-throat-and-scalp-you" Injun eyes focused right on him. Of all those involved, Luther blamed the boy the least, had even liked him in a way, or at least admired how he'd been such a quick study with the cards.

Luther nodded toward the necklace, closed his eyes, and shook his head. "Please let me explain what happened. When I see that necklace, my blood boils and I lose my mind. If you can believe it, I actually came here to apologize. Then my thoughts turned to the necklace, and it was like the devil himself was in me."

Ezekiel spoke, "No, we don't believe that for a second. Belle told me that you paid her to keep me away. Why would you do that if you'd come to apologize? And look." He pointed to Ophelia's neck and battered face. "That doesn't look like an apology. I will take great pleasure in killing you slowly and painfully. And when I'm done, I'll chop you up into bite-sized pieces for the dogs and cats on Fifth Street."

"Not the dogs please." Luther lifted his hand and shook his head. "Listen, that necklace has a devilish power over me. For the most part, I'm a good man. Ask my wife."

"I was going to kill you anyway—for raping my sister."

"For doing what?" Luther looked at Ophelia with disappointment and pity. "Is that what you told him? Is that really what you think happened? Oh, you poor, deluded girl. The attack was too much. I've heard of things like this happening to girls after brutal attacks by highwaymen and savages. Well, that explains why you shot me. I could never figure that out."

Her eyes were wide. She didn't move and barely blinked. She just stared into the distance with a stunned, vacant expression. Luther cleared his throat. "Admittedly, I was a coward. When the Indians came, I hid in a bush. I watched them drag you off. They raided the place and left. I found you lying facedown in the river, fortunately, you were still breathing. I carried you home. Do you remember that?"

She closed her eyes and shook her head violently. "No. No. You lie!" she yelled. She kept her eyes closed. Her breathing was deep and audible. Her chest heaved. "I keep trying to spare your life, to convince myself that killing would be wrong. But you're making it so hard, and I'm beginning to think that deep down, you're vile and evil and poisonous to the world and everyone in it."

Luther nodded at her in a sympathetic manner, as if she were ill. "I'm sure it's easier to blame me than remember the horror of what actually happened. Did you ask your brother about his dealings with Black Hawk? I pray to God that wasn't part of the deal. It's hard to believe someone would do that to his own kin. I'm sure that wasn't part of his plan. Sadly, you just can't trust the Indians. They're not like us."

He had planned none of this. And yet the words came so easily, just slid off his tongue in such a convincing manner. Divide and conquer. He was surprised his brain worked so well after the blow to his head. He looked at the glass in front of him and licked his lips. "Do you think I could have a little drink? My throat is parched."

They ignored his request. Ophelia turned to her brother. "What did happen with you and Black Hawk?" she asked softly. "I didn't realize you'd ever met with him."

Clearly ashamed, Ezekiel looked at the ground and answered. "I was trying to plan our escape, and we needed a better horse, so I told him where the granary cache was and traded a few belongings. But that's it. I never thought they would—"

She shook her head. "No, they didn't. It wasn't the Indians, Ezekiel. He's lying. That's what he does. And the tragedy is that

I thought we could find out the truth, about Mother, about the necklace, about you and your father. That we'd let him live so he could tell us about all this." She gestured to the picture, the letter, his book, and the necklace lying on the table like clues to a crime. "But he's just proven himself completely untrustworthy, a liar to the core. You can kill him. Give him a drink before he dies." She gestured to the glass in a resigned and disappointed manner.

Luther realized he'd gone too far. "Ophelia, please, whether you believe the lie or the truth, the hurt is still there. Let me be a liar then, if that eases your suffering. Yes, it was me, your dear uncle, and not a pack of savages that dragged you off into the night. Now listen, I'll tell you the story of that necklace, and your mother, and the tragedy that destroyed our lives. Maybe you'll finally understand what comes over me when I see it. But you mustn't kill me. There's a special place in hell for people who kill their own kin, and I don't want either of you to end up there."

They stared at him. "Well go on then," Ophelia finally said, looking at the items on the table.

He cleared his throat and nodded at the drink. She slid it in front of him. They watched him lap it like a dog; his desire for the liquor was stronger than his pride. Unable to drink the rest, he looked at the glass in defeat and gave them a pleading look.

Ophelia sighed and nodded to Zeke, indicating he should assist Luther. Ezekiel grudgingly lifted the cup, held it to Luther's lips, and poured the rest of the liquor down his throat without care. Luther licked his lips and chin, trying to get the last drops.

"Okay," he said, feeling the spirits. "Where should I start?" He looked at the objects on the table as if they were tarot cards.

Twenty-Six

Ophelia glanced at the letter and the picture that had fallen from the pages of Luther's worn diary. Ezekiel let out a bored sigh and casually unsheathed the knife he strapped to his ankle. He studied the blade and then Luther, as if devising a plan on how to best butcher him.

Luther watched Ezekiel with an expression of fear and dread. "If you want me to tell you the story, you have to promise not to kill me," he said.

Ophelia and Ezekiel looked at each other, then back at him without answering.

"Or at least, give me the mercy of a bullet," he said, looking at the knife with revulsion.

Ophelia nodded at Ezekiel and the knife. "Put it away, please," she said softly, and turned her attention back to Luther. She picked up the letter. "This is addressed to a Thomas Cashman and begins: 'Dear Thomas.' Who is Thomas? And how did you end up with this letter?"

Luther looked like there was a bad taste in his mouth. "Thomas was a spoiled baby and a big, unpleasant surprise to all of us. Nearly killed my mother. After your mother and I were disowned, he was the only heir to Father's estate. I don't know what happened to him. Maybe he died. I have no knowledge of that, but someone forwarded this letter to me in Missouri. You see, it was fate."

Ophelia looked at him in disgust. She was fighting a war

within herself, battling all of her anger and instincts not to let Ezekiel kill him. But everything she experienced in her proximity to death had solidified her conviction that killing was wrong.

Ophelia read the address. "Thomas Cashman, Fourteen Sea Street, Newburyport, Massachusetts."

"Yes, that was our address. A grand house. Father was a successful merchant. And I was being groomed as his successor—until your mother destroyed everything."

"Look, Zeke." Ophelia handed her brother the letter. "This is Mother's writing."

Zeke looked at it and nodded, but his attention was fixed on the picture of the Indian school. He handed it back to her. "Read it aloud," he said.

"My throat hurts and my voice is hoarse. Would you?" She handed him the letter.

With grave concern, Zeke moved her hair, looked at her neck, and then shot Luther a disgusted, murderous glare. He squinted down at the letter. Then, as if he'd been caught doing something wrong, he looked up at Ophelia. "I know what you're thinking, and I don't need spectacles. My eyes just need to adjust." He cleared his throat.

Dearest Thomas,

I hope this letter finds you, and also finds you in good health. My shame and disownment are the reason for my lack of past correspondence. You were just a baby when the "unfortunate incident" occurred, and I'm not sure if you remember me, or even know of my existence. Your brother, Luther, was very angry with me for my grave error in judgment that was in reality a matter of my heart overtaking reason. Sadly, the wrath and shame I brought upon the family extended to him, and he was also cast out and disowned. I would not be troubling you with my memories and the scandal I caused, except that my time on earth is almost over, and I believe my husband's death is also imminent, as we have both contracted the same disease.

I was fortunate to find a religion, Mormonism, and a man, Harold Oatman, who accepted me despite my fallen state. The truth is, if Luther hadn't intervened, I would have ended up a prisoner in an asylum. Except for the child in my womb, I was completely alone in the world. To escape persecution and start a new life, I joined the Mormons and soon after that, met Mr. Oatman. Along with hundreds of others, we made the arduous journey by wagon train to the Utah Territory in the land we call Zion. Not soon after we arrived, the second prophet, Brigham Young, sent us to the southwest desert to grow cotton.

Our lives in the desert have been trying but love and faith have seen us through. I do not fear death. I fear for the children I leave behind, particularly my daughter, Ophelia. Although the Mormons saved me, I do not wish my daughter to become a polygamist's wife, especially without the guiding hand of her father to choose her a husband. Her brother, Ezekiel, as a half-breed, is rather a lost soul, but he is strong and independent and has an affinity for survival in the wilderness. My only regret is that he will never know his tribe, the Cherokee, who are a proud, intelligent people, and his father, who never caused me injury, and whom I truly loved, although our love was forbidden.

I have harped on enough about the past. My reason for writing is to beg you to have mercy on my daughter, Ophelia. If you would agree to be her guardian, we could arrange her passage to Boston. She will possess a family heirloom, which Mother gave me the night I left. It should be sufficient to pay for her keep until marriage or employment is secured. Ezekiel is almost a man, and he cares a great deal for his sister, but because of his mixed race, I foresee trouble in this sphere.

If you are craving the adventure of a lifetime, the vast frontier holds natural wonders and majesty your eyes will scarcely believe. The trail has much improved since our trek, and there are many reputable stage companies and stations along the way. The journey is best undertaken at the beginning of May, after danger of snow, and before the summer heat. Our home is not luxurious and can't be compared to our childhood home. Yet the land has a spirit, no matter what your religion, that is indescribable and incomparable to anything I knew in youth.

I do miss the sight and smell of the ocean, the summer clam and lobster bakes, and the fragrant woods, among other things. I regret that I will never see any of it, or any of the Cashman clan, again. If you could find it in your heart to forgive, not for my sake, but for the sake of your niece, I implore you to send a letter to this settlement so that we can make arrangements to send her to Boston by rail.

Yours truly,
Sarah Bridget Oatman

Ezekiel stopped reading, sniffed, blinked, and picked up the picture. It felt like their mother was in the room with them.

Ophelia got up and retrieved a magnifying glass from a kitchen drawer. "I know you don't need spectacles. But that picture is old and blurry."

He looked annoyed but took the magnifier and peered closer at the photo, focusing on his father. "That was Mother's voice, wasn't it?" She picked up the letter and imagined her mother writing it. Now she had something of her mother's other than the cursed necklace.

"You see," said Luther. "Right there in that letter she says I saved her from the asylum. If it weren't for me, you never would've been born." He looked at Ezekiel. "And Lord knows what would've become of you."

Incredulous, Ophelia stared at Luther, then looked down at the letter, and emphatically reread the most salient line. "She will possess a family heirloom, which Mother gave me the night I left." She waited for some sign of comprehension, but Luther looked blank and stunned. "Mother gave me," stressed Ophelia. "You see, my mother didn't steal the necklace. Her mother—your mother—gave it to her."

Luther's eyes watered, and he started convulsing with grief. They watched as he deteriorated, much the same way as he had when he first saw the necklace. His grand display of emotion made them uncomfortable. Ezekiel poured himself another drink. And this time Ophelia poured herself liquor rather than lemon water. She splashed a little more into Luther's glass, but in his fit of grief and rage, he didn't even notice.

"My own mother! She betrayed me! She told Father I stole the necklace, when all along she'd given it to Bridget!" He slammed his fist on the table as rage overtook his grief. "Why would she do that? Why? Why? Why?" he screamed. "She ruined my life!"

"I don't know," said Ophelia, feeling the first tiny speck of pity. She slid the glass toward him. "Tell us the whole story from the beginning, and maybe we can figure out her reasons."

Ezekiel passed her the tattered picture. In it, a group of Indian children posed in front of a schoolhouse. At one end of the group her mother stood, and at the other end stood an Indian-looking man in a suit, who must've been the schoolmaster and Ezekiel's father.

Twenty-Seven

Luther's tears and snot dripped on to the old oaken table. More from disgust than compassion, Ophelia pinched a handkerchief from his coat pocket and tossed it in front of him. As his hands were still bound, the handkerchief was no help. Powerless and broken, he looked at the liquor and the handkerchief and began to cry again, harder, as if they represented all the injustices of his life.

"I was so ambitious. I would've tripled Father's business. I would've built an empire if it weren't for your damned mother. Why did she have to come to Virginia with me? She ruined everything."

Zeke stood, grabbed him by the throat, and squeezed. "Tell the story without insulting our mother," he said and let go.

Luther's eyes bulged. He coughed, wheezed, and panted.

"See what it feels like?" said Ezekiel. "Not too good. Ask Ophelia."

Luther gave Zeke a menacing glare, but then he seemed to remember the knife and that these two would decide whether he lived and how he'd die. The clock chimed. It was midnight. A breeze filled the house, and rain tapped on the windows. He raised his brows and looked around, confused, as if the noise was a cue to commence with his judgment and sentencing.

"I apologize," he said. "After you hear this story, you'll see I'm the real victim, and my anger is justified."

Ophelia coughed and rolled her eyes. "Zeke, would you untie

one of his hands, so he can wipe his disgusting face. At this rate, it'll be morning before we get through this." The rain tapped harder. "I'm going to run upstairs and shut the windows. It sounds like a storm's coming."

Luther wiped his face and nose, then blotted the blood from his head with the handkerchief.

"I'll go," said Zeke. "You need to rest after your ordeal." He picked up the rope to retie Luther's hand. Luther noticed and downed the liquor as fast as he could.

Ophelia didn't want to be alone in the same room as Luther, so she went on the porch while Ezekiel was shutting the windows. The heat had finally broken, and the rain smelled sweet and clean. She went back down and sat at the table where Ezekiel was drumming his fingers and Luther was looking like a devious overgrown child, one who should never have been born.

He cleared his throat and spoke. "I was about to embark on a business trip for Father to negotiate some contracts in the south. Bridget had just finished her studies, and she begged to accompany me. Tensions were rising between the north and south. I told her that if she came, she'd have to keep a lid on all her abolitionist talk. She agreed, but as soon as we arrived and she saw the plantation slaves, it was all I could do to make her shut her trap. We were the guests of a prominent family and were supposed to stay on their plantation for three months. She caused so much controversy with all her political talk. There was a temporary opening for a teacher at a nearby Indian Day School, and I suggested she apply. That way I could continue my negotiations without her causing trouble." He nodded to the picture of the school. "That's it there."

Ophelia picked up the magnifying glass and held it over the tiny blurred face of her mother.

"On one end is your mother. And—" He looked at Ezekiel. "On the other end is your father. He was a Cherokee, a learned man, dedicated to the education of his people. But then he had the misfortune of meeting Bridget."

Ezekiel made a sudden angry movement.

Luther flinched and put up his hand. "Okay, I'm sorry. She was staying in the modest teacher's quarters next to the school. And I was busy with business. By the time I got out to see her, it was too late—so much for keeping her out of trouble. Three months later, there she was with child and blind with love for the Indian schoolmaster. She claimed they'd been married in some kind of ceremony. But as far as I could tell, it wasn't legal. I had to forcibly drag her away." He sighed and shook his head. "In order to get her back to Newburyport, I finally had to sedate her.

"After we got home and Father found out, he was livid. He blamed me because I was her older brother, and I was supposed to look after her. His main concern was hiding her away before anyone found out she was with child. More than family, he cared about family reputation, about appearances. He couldn't bare the shame of his prized daughter becoming a fallen woman. We visited a home for wayward girls and spoke to the warden. I'd heard of these places, but I'd never visited one. It was horrific. And as mad as I was at Bridget, I didn't think she deserved such a fate. I tried to dissuade Father, but he'd made up his mind, and he signed the papers that day. He told me it was my responsibility to get her there, even if I had to use force."

He paused, cleared his throat, and gave them his most earnest look. "Now, when you consider what to do with me, consider this: I told Bridget about Father's plan. I gave her all my savings. And the day I was supposed to have her imprisoned in that place, I took her to the train station instead. I told her to buy a one-way ticket somewhere and disappear. I risked my future so she could escape. The home for wayward girls wasn't a home. It was a prison of the worst variety. And I had a strong premonition that once she entered, she'd never leave. When we visited, I heard screams and saw ghastly expressions on the poor girls' faces." He shook his head at the memory.

"But looking back, I should've done what father wanted. He discovered the ruby necklace was missing and asked Mother about it. She told him she had no idea what had happened to it. He assumed it was me. I was certain Bridget had stolen it, and I was enraged that she'd steal it after everything I'd done to help her. Now I see that it was Mother who gave it to Bridget and then lied to Father. Mother and Bridget were very close. Bridget must've told her about our plans. I suppose Mother gave her the necklace to sell because she didn't have any money. Father kept her on a strict allowance. Anyway, when Father found out Bridget never arrived at the home, he blamed me and also concluded that I'd stolen the necklace. Not only was I disowned, but he also reported me to the police, so I became a fugitive. That's how I ended up in the south."

"What happened to my father? What was his name?" Ezekiel asked.

"Huh? His name? His name was—uh. I can't think of it now. But I will, and maybe I can help you find him, or at least locate his tribe."

"Why should we believe anything you say?" asked Ezekiel.

Ophelia had been thinking the exact same thing. He'd lied about everything else. Why would he tell the truth about this?

Luther sat up, straightened in his chair, and tried to appear as dignified as he could with his hands tied. "Most men put in this situation would've had your father arrested," he said to Ezekiel.

"So, why didn't you?" Zeke asked.

Luther cleared his throat and bobbed his head. "Well, now, don't take this as an insult to your mother, but I knew her very well. Ever since I can remember I'd been tasked with trying to make her behave. And she was always—well, I don't want to insult her, so I'll just say she had a strong will and a mind of her own. She followed her passions without thinking of the repercussions. I'm sure she loved your father. And I'm also quite sure she willingly threw herself into his arms. Southerners don't have much patience for the courts, and considering he was Indian, I figured he'd be lynched. So I dragged Bridget away kicking and screaming, but I didn't say anything to anyone about why I did it."

The girl he was describing sounded nothing like their quiet, stoic mother. Ophelia supposed she'd been different before life broke her spirit.

"So I saved your father's life as well, and that's why I think you should spare mine. As you see, this whole ordeal, even now, has driven me to the brink of insanity."

Ophelia looked at Ezekiel and wondered if he was thinking what she was thinking. "Well," she said, and drummed the table in finality. "Then maybe you should spend some time in an asylum. That's probably a much better solution than killing you. We'll make the arrangements tomorrow. I've heard enough."

"You mean like one of the sanatoriums with the thermal springs?" he asked.

Ophelia smiled, and her eyes filled with amusement. "No," she said and shook her head. "Ezekiel, please make sure he's tightly bound. In his unstable condition, we don't want him to escape and hurt anyone else."

Zeke took some extra rope and began to bind Luther's legs to the chair.

"Wait! I'm to stay here, like this, all night?" he cried.

Zeke finished, put out the kitchen gas lamp, and he and Ophelia walked out of the room together.

"But I have to relieve myself," he called.

Ezekiel put his arm around Ophelia and closed the kitchen door.

Twenty-Eight

With a bruised neck and battered face, Ophelia boarded the train to Denver. She didn't have time to wait for her wounds to heal. The emptiness of Charlie's absence hurt more than her injuries. By now he'd have realized the telegram had been a hoax. The unfortunate possibility that he'd already boarded a train back to Ogden, and that she'd miss him in transit, occurred to her as her head bounced, bobbed, and jerked in rhythm with the train's movement.

She had the address of his old boarding house—the one where she'd first contacted him when she had inquired about hiring him to find Ezekiel. It seemed like so long ago, but it hadn't even been a year. Once she arrived in Denver, she hailed a hack directly from the station to the boarding house, hoping he'd be there. She had a small coach bag, nothing to suggest she was on a long journey or going to stay anywhere for long, yet the landlady gave her a cold, unwelcoming stare as she walked in the front door.

"Sorry, ma'am, men only," she said and pointed to a sign by the door.

"Oh, I'm not looking for lodging. I'm trying to locate my brother, Charles Sirringo."

The lady noticed Ophelia's battered face and softened. "Yes, he's still here. But he's scheduled to leave this afternoon before dinner, so you're lucky you came today. He went out for something, but I think he'll be back shortly. Ah, let's see . . . I suppose it's all right if you wait in the study there. But females aren't allowed upstairs." She pointed to a room lined with bookshelves and old mismatched chairs.

"Thank you," said Ophelia. She sat down, put her bag on her lap, and sighed in relief. She read the book titles and tried to calm the fluttering in her stomach by focusing on them instead of rehearsing what she'd say to Charlie, which she'd already done repeatedly on the seven-hundred-mile trip from Ogden.

About fifteen minutes later the door rattled opened, and she heard Charlie's voice. "My sister?" He looked in the parlor, saw her, and winked. "Ah, my sister. You're not Chinese anymore," he said and grinned.

Ophelia put her bag on the floor and stood. He held out his arms and embraced her in a much more intimate manner than one would embrace a sibling. The landlady looked at them, puzzled and suspicious. "Ah, my sister," he said and squeezed her again. Then he noticed her face and his expression changed. "What the—" He glanced over his shoulder at the landlady. She lowered her eyes and left the room. He saw the bruises on Ophelia's neck and craned his head sideways to get a better look. He winced, and then his eyes filled with fury.

"What happened? Who did this?"

"Is there somewhere private we can talk?" she asked.

He looked around. "Yes, um . . ." He went into the hallway and checked to see if the landlady was around. "Females aren't allowed upstairs, but I think she's gone off to cook dinner. Besides, everyone breaks that rule, and I'm leaving today anyway. Come on," he whispered and took her bag.

They tiptoed up the stairs and went into his room. She sat in a chair. He paced the small room, then kneeled and inspected her face and neck. He focused on her neck. "These are fingerprints," he said. "Who did this? What happened?"

"First, I have to tell you that when you heard me proposition-ing Mr. Topham, it was only to get him away from the root cellar because Ezekiel and Belle were in there, right in the middle of—the act."

"Yes, I believe you. I'm sorry I doubted you. I should never have left. Please, Ophelia, tell me who did this."

"Luther," she said.

His face froze and then fell, and he looked sad, guilty, and furious.

"Charlie, he fools a lot of people. You believed his lies, didn't you?"

He sat on the bed next to his half-packed bag and held his head in his hands. "How could I fall for him? I'm a seasoned detective, and you warned me about him as well. He convinced me you were deluded. That the Indian attack had made you mentally feeble and that you'd imagined it was him who raped you instead."

Ophelia cocked her head to the side. "Indian attack," she said skeptically.

He stared at her, shocked. "Yes, I know, that's the oldest trick in the book. Highwaymen blaming Indians, even going as far as dressing like them . . . how could I fall for that? I'm so sorry."

"You've told me many stories of how you infiltrated gangs of outlaws and anarchists. And when they found out you weren't one of them, they were shocked. You acted so convincingly, they couldn't believe you weren't one of them, even when they knew better. Well, I guess you share something in common with Luther. He's very bad. But he's a good actor, and he can trick people. That's what makes him so dangerous. He's a charlatan." She pulled the telegram from her pocket and handed it to him.

He shook it in the air. "I looked everywhere for this. The Pinkerton office said they knew nothing about it." He peered at it, stood, and went to the window for better light, where he inspected it for a minute, and then shook his head in disgust.

"A forgery—I was duped."

"Luther sent that to lure you away. Then he went to Belle and promised her a handsome sum if she'd keep Ezekiel at her place for the night. I have no idea how he found out about us, but it probably wasn't too difficult, since I've been using my legal name instead of an alias. That was quite stupid on my part. Belle and Ezekiel have an especially close relationship, which perhaps explains why they were entangled in the root cellar. Luckily, she told Ezekiel about Luther. Unfortunately for me, he'd already done some damage by the time she got around to it." She gestured to her face.

He stared at the floor intently, then he looked around the room as if he were searching for missing details. "Can you tell me exactly what happened, or is that too painful?"

Ophelia sighed, nodded, and closed her eyes. "I was alone in the house and very sad because you were gone. Ezekiel was supposed to be at Belle's for the night." Her voice became high-pitched and her body tensed, as if a hundred knives were going into her. Then she shook and sobbed uncontrollably.

Charlie came over and guided her to sit on the bed. He sat, too, held her, and whispered, "Shhh, shhh. It's all right now. I shouldn't have left. I'm so sorry."

She nodded and sniffed and tried to compose herself. "Okay, okay. I'm okay. So I was sitting on the roof with a bottle of brandy, feeling really bad for myself. I even thought about jumping but was afraid it wasn't high enough to kill me."

"Oh, Ophelia," he said and squeezed her.

"It's all right. It was just a thought, and not something I'd ever do. Anyway, I came in through the window and there he was. He was angry and wanted the necklace. I kicked him and tried to run, but that made him angrier, and he grabbed me by the throat. And I was trying to tell him that the necklace was inside my old doll, but I couldn't talk because he was choking me, so I pointed and pointed. He thought I was pointing to the pillow, so he ripped that open, and then he started choking me again, and I thought he was going to kill me, but I managed to point again, and he finally understood that I was pointing to the doll. He ripped her apart. When he found the necklace, he started to shake and tremble and cry, much the same way as I just did, except he fell to his knees and started screaming at his mother. It was the strangest behavior from a grown man. I passed out. I think I might have been dead or something because what I saw . . . I'll tell you more about that later. When I came to, Ezekiel was there, and Luther was lying on the floor bleeding from his head.

"We found some pictures and a letter in his pocket. He knew Ezekiel wanted to kill him, so he tried to curry favor. He told him Indians had attacked and carried me off that night. Right in front of me, he told that lie. Claimed he hid in a bush and then carried me from the river. Probably the same story he told you." She sighed and shook her head. "It put into question everything he said after. But the manner in which he wept and carried on, dripping snot and buckets of tears, I don't think even the best actor could pull off a performance like that. Anyway, we found out about my mother and Ezekiel's father, who was a Cherokee schoolteacher. They were in love. You can probably guess how that turned out for them."

Charlie raised his eyebrows. "Not very well."

"Exactly," said Ophelia. "Apparently, she was feisty and disobedient back then. Luther blames her for everything. When he found out she was with child, he dragged her back to Massachusetts. That's where they came from. Their father was a wealthy merchant. He was furious and arranged for Mother to be committed to some kind of home for wayward girls. Luther said it was more like a prison. He was supposed to bring her there, but after he saw the place, he said he felt bad and showed her mercy. According to him, he gave her his savings and dropped her off at a railroad station. It turned out the mother knew what was happening and gave her the necklace. But when the father discovered the rubies were missing and found out Luther helped Mother escape, he blamed Luther for everything, even stealing the necklace. Their mother didn't stick up for him. I guess she was too scared of their father. Anyway, their father not only disowned him, but also reported him to the police. So Luther basically became a fugitive, went to the south, and got lost in his bitterness, the war, and God knows what else. And that's how he became the monster he is today." She shuddered as she thought of the inseparable broth of truth and lies that had poured out of him like the runs. "Ugh," she said, "I feel sick now."

"So what did Ezekiel do with the body," whispered Charlie.

"What?"

A loud knock made Ophelia jump. The landlady called through the closed door, "Mr. Sirringo, are you there? Is your sister there with you? Remember the rules, please. No females upstairs, even if they claim to be relations."

"Very well, yes, of course. She's just helping me pack my bag. We'll be right down."

The landlady made a loud, exasperated noise and then thumped back down the stairs.

"How did Zeke get rid of Luther's body?" Charlie whispered again.

"He didn't kill him, Charlie."

"What? Why not? Where the hell is he? I'm going to kill him."

"No more killing, Charlie. Don't worry. He's safely locked away in a lunatic asylum. I even got his wife's permission."

"What? Ophelia, he was trying to kill you. At the very least, he should be in the penitentiary."

"Yeah, well, Ezekiel and I aren't too fond of dealing with the law for obvious reasons. Wait, there's one thing more." She fished in her pocket, pulled out the little girl's picture, and held it out to him.

He took it and looked at it sadly. "I was looking for this, too."

"I found it under the bed. Is that the picture you were looking at in Frisco? Who is she?"

He walked over to the window and looked out. "There's something I haven't told you, or rather, lied to you about. I was married once. My wife died when our daughter was a baby. I couldn't take care of her, so I sent her to some of my wife's relatives. Every month, I paid them for her upkeep. But I fell on hard times, and I missed some payments. By the time I could make it up, they'd already sent her to an orphanage. I failed to protect her like I failed to protect you and my sister." He kept his back to her, but Ophelia could feel his remorse and deep sadness. She'd thought he seemed a little too experienced sexually and was glad all of his experience wasn't acquired in brothels. But she felt terrible about him losing his daughter.

"Charlie, why didn't you tell me? I owe you money. I have the money. We'll get her. I can take care of her. What's her name?"

"Viola." He turned and faced Ophelia. She saw fear in his eyes. "What if something bad has already happened to her?"

"Don't worry. What happened to me won't happen to her. And even if you were there for her, nothing in this world can protect a little girl—or even a boy. All children fall. It's just a matter of how hard, and how broken they get. When I was a child, my two best friends from Grafton fell from a tree while they were swinging. They were swinging and singing, as innocent as pie, then the branch broke, then they were falling, and then they were dead." She sniffed at the memory, and her eyes watered. "Maybe the children who don't make it float away like spring cotton to a better place, and they don't ever have to worry about being hurt or broken again."

"Mr. Sirringo!" the landlady called.

Charlie hugged Ophelia and threw the rest of his stuff into his travel case. She grabbed her bag, and they raced down the stairs and out the front door. They walked west, hands joined, toward the train station where the sky was pink and fiery with sunset.

Twenty-Nine

The courtyard was designed to instill tranquility in the patients—lots of grass and shrubs, trees, even a small pond stocked with goldfish. Yet Luther was anything but tranquil. He wore the necklace. It was tight around his thick neck, like a choker collar. And even though it caused him great discomfort, it was his albatross to bear, and he refused to let them remove it.

"Let him wear it then," the doctor conceded.

His hands and feet were bound with humane leather straps. They'd said it was for his safety. When he screamed, they wheeled him to a far corner of the courtyard, left him alone, and closed the doors. He watched the fish dart about in the small artificial pond, as much prisoners as he was. He tried to spit at them but failed. Only the birds were free.

A visitor—an old woman wrapped in a deep burgundy shawl—came through the doors and out to the courtyard. Despite her age, she had a stately countenance. She left a younger middle-aged man who accompanied her and approached him alone, walking slowly and leaning on her cane as she made her way across the verdant grass. Luther felt both hope and fear. Sweat poured down his temples as he struggled to free his arms and legs. She stopped three feet away and looked him up and down.

"Luther? Is that you? Why are you wearing that necklace? I

gave it to your sister."

"Take it off," he screamed and sobbed. "Take it off!"

ABOUT THE AUTHOR

Alison L. McLennan was born and raised in Quincy, Massachusetts. She moved to Utah in 1989 and earned an undergraduate degree at the University of Utah. One of the main characters in her debut novel, *Falling for Johnny,* was inspired by the infamous James "Whitey" Bulger. *Falling for Johnny* won an honorable mention in the 2012 Utah Original Writing Competition and the 2013 Inkubate Literary Blockbuster Challenge. She earned an MFA from the Solstice Program, where she was awarded a fellowship for fiction. *Ophelia's War* was first written as her creative thesis. In 2019, she traveled to Nepal, did a solo trek in the Himalaya and became a certified Kundalini Yoga Teacher. She's currently working on *Falling Awake,* a novel based on near-death experiences and spiritual transformations.

The employees of Five Star Publishing hope you have enjoyed this book.

Our Five Star novels explore little-known chapters from America's history, stories told from unique perspectives that will entertain a broad range of readers.

Other Five Star books are available at your local library, bookstore, all major book distributors, and directly from Five Star/Gale.

Connect with Five Star Publishing

Visit us on Facebook:
https://www.facebook.com/FiveStarCengage

Email:
FiveStar@cengage.com

For information about titles and placing orders:
(800) 223-1244
gale.orders@cengage.com

To share your comments, write to us:
Five Star Publishing
Attn: Publisher
10 Water St., Suite 310
Waterville, ME 04901